The Elias Chronicles~BOOK III

THE ELIXIR:
JOURNEY ON

BOOKS BY E. G. KARDOS

ZEN MASTER NEXT DOOR:

Parables for Enlightened Everyday Living

THE ELIAS CHRONICLES

The Amulet: Journey to Sirok~ Book I

The Rings: Journey Beneath Sirok~ Book II

The Elixir: Journey On- Book III

CUTTING OF HARP STRINGS: a novel

The Elias Chronicles~BOOK III

THE ELIXIR: JOURNEY ON

E.G. Kardos

First Edition 2024
PEN IT PUBLICATIONS

Published by Pen It Publications in the U.S.A.

713-526-3989

www.penitpublications.com

ISBN: 978-1-63984-520-0

Edited by Ashlee Wyzard

Cover Design by Donna Cook

For Matt C.

CONTENTS

A gem cannot be polished without friction, nor a man perfected without trials.

Seneca.

The black moment is the moment when the real message of transformation is going to come. At the darkest moment comes the light.

Joseph Campbell

1

An Unexpected Treasure

The razor-sharp splinters of the wet deck jutted into his cheek, but he didn't feel any pain. He felt nothing. Seemingly more dead than alive, he lay motionless and face down, with his limp arms stretched outward. He was alone.

Hours passed before life seeped back into his body, and he began to sense a steady and gentle rocking as a dank and thick breeze kicked up and gave him a shudder. This revived him but only gave him a blurred world to make sense of. He shut his eyes, hoping that the next time he opened them, all would be clear. His body felt like a bag of rocks. He groaned, and as he did, he twisted his face like the coil of a spring in an old watch. Like the last puff of air out of an inner tube, he let out a sigh. Eyes painfully closed, he pulled one arm down close to his tender ribs, and, bearing weight on his side, he grimaced and awkwardly rolled over onto his back.

The whooshing sound of the cold, dark water slapped against the rotting, gray planks that bound him on all sides like a large coffin. Its walls were doing all they could to separate him from the murky unknown. An occasional spray whipped up and whirled about, and this time, a few random droplets landed on his lips, stirring his senses and waking his need for water. Instinctually reaching with his tongue, he tasted the whole sea in those tiny beads of life. Inhaling, he filled his lungs with wafts of the salty air, causing him a tinge of confusion but kindling much more curiosity that his mind wasn't yet ready to dare unravel. His eyelids fluttered as he opened his eyes wide again, only this time to focus on the buttery and crimson-laced clouds that draped like streamers overhead. Still bewildered and in a muddle about his whereabouts, he listlessly reached up as if to touch the layers of clouds. As he did, they mysteriously drew apart from each other, and much like cotton candy, they left their curling and wispy remains that faded on the edges.

"Am I...could I be—home?"

He sluggishly sat up, and as he did, he expanded his ribcage and stretched his shoulder blades backward. Rubbing one shoulder and then the next, he rotated his head back and forth. Somberly, he carefully rubbed his cheek, brushing away flecks of the ancient lifeboat. He found reassurance when he touched his chest to find his amulet still hanging from his neck. Moving his thoughts outward, he couldn't believe where he was as his eyes grew twice their normal size as his surroundings, just then, slapped him into reality.

He hastily looked about as his torso straightened. Pricks of sweat beads pierced his face, and his heart pumped at full throttle. Jerking his head from starboard to bow, he saw only the calm shadowy sea and a soupy mist, making him feel all sides were moving in on him in what, he thought, was an endless and cruel sea. As the clouds tugged themselves apart even more or burned off by the rising heat of the sun, like surly rapids surging over boulders, contrasting thoughts bounded in his aching head. He jumped to his feet, nearly capsizing the craft. From his gut and roaring up to his lips, he screamed out to the vast sea that imprisoned him.

"WHERE AM I?"

The endless wrinkles of each wave devoured his cry, and a rush of panic overcame him as he dropped to his knees and, in a shaky whisper, said, "This is not home." Trying to make sense of his whereabouts, exploding up, he rushed from port to starboard, surveying the cold, ghostly waters.

"Kelsa! Zoltan! Cimbora! ANYBODY! WHERE ARE YOU? That portal was supposed to be our ticket home. What happened? Are you out there? ANYONE!"

Elias furiously scanned all he could see in every direction and then shook his head as he dug his fingers into his temples and looked to the deck.

"How? How did this happen? HOW?" in awe, he asked under his breath. Looking one way and then darting his head toward the other, he shouted, "LANTOS—GASPAR, are you out there? ANYBODY?" He paused and heard nothing in return. All was eerily quiet. He blurted out again, "Lantos...Gaspar...it's no use...no use." He was alone.

He staggered backward and collapsed on a small, rickety bench. He leaned forward and supported his head in his soft, boyish hands with his elbows on his knees. His long dark hair flopped forward, covering his face.

Interrogating himself, he asked aloud, "What did I do wrong? What could have happened? Where am I?" Answering himself, he continued, "I somehow landed in this, this tiny boat on a huge sea, and everyone else...I mean, everyone else must be—must be...dead," his words softened as he gazed at the planks under his battered boots and shook his head in disbelief. "Where *IS* everyone?" he cried as he felt the sharp and bitter sting of loneliness shoot throughout his body.

In absolute shock, he collapsed, crumpling back onto the deck where he lay only moments earlier. His gut tightened, and the sensation turned to a hollowness that penetrated his chest. His heart hurt. As it did, he felt cold as a shiver ran through his veins to every muscle. Although the sea now smacked against the boat, the sound and vibration meant nothing to him. In and out of the clouds, the sun began to throw its radiance like shards of a broken mirror on the unrelenting waves. Although his eyes were wide open, he saw nothing. His thoughts were detached from his body. Numb—he was despondent—more than any time in his sixteen years.

Moments turned to hours as he lay on his back, fully conscious but motionless. Fixing his gaze to the heavens, he seemed to melt into every crevasse of the porous and splintered deck. His thoughts turned to Ordak's evil curse on him that he withstood during his banishment to the red and dusty desert known as the Forsaken Sea. It looped in his consciousness. Ordak, he surmised, must be behind this detour, but as soon as he thought it, he immediately blotted the notion out of his head so as not to use his energy on the negative. He knew the negative was a ravenous shark that would mercilessly eat him whole with one mighty chomp. He remembered this from his brief stay with Tas, the mystic who taught him about his powers using the Endless Within—a power all humans have, but few seldom use. "Yeah, right... I have *the gift*...the *Donum*. Look at me. I'm the *one* who's supposed to be *the one*. Yeah, right! I'm in a boat in the middle of the sea!"

Time passed, and he raised his hand and rested it on his chest. Without so much as a thought, he stoically began to play with the amulet. With his fingers, he swirled it on his chest, occasionally flipping it over. Still focused on the blend of colors in the sky and with no central thought in his head, he held the small medallion between his thumb and the side of his index finger. At that very instant, not a second later, he smiled as something happened, and a force deep inside of him began to stir his core. Like waking from a deep sleep, he was unexpectedly refreshed as he recognized a specific force, and it came from a tiny spark well hidden inside that was real and a part of his very being.

"Enough of this—I'm in a lifeboat. A LIFEBOAT—LIFE!" He drove new thoughts to mind, and they were positive thoughts he had overlooked only a minute earlier. As the warm flicker of a flame melts a candle, so the thumping in his chest vibrated throughout his body and deadened any pain that he suffered—real or perceived. Elias began to warm, and he allowed this sense to take charge. He knew his sulking and despondence would not offer him the answers he wanted or needed. Instead of looking outside, he now remembered and understood that everything must come from his own resolve—*The Endless Within*. His survival and his life were in his own hands, and the faster he acted, the faster he knew he would find his friends and his way home. In doing so, he knew he would uncover the reason for this new quest, like it or not, and that this momentary roundabout route would somehow make sense.

Refocused on the lifeboat and all its contents, he knew he must determine if anything on this tiny vessel could give him a clue to all that was now swimming in his head. With newfound worth, he sat up to study all that was close around him—all that he could touch and figure out to use.

The boat was small but could accommodate eighteen to twenty passengers nestled close together based on the dilapidated benches that remained loosely intact. Looking over the rig, he saw a thick rope lying curled like the thread of a screw. Beside it, he saw one ten-foot oar that was no longer fastened to either of the two oarlocks. The lone oar lay on the deck to one side and, to the stern, was a large wooden box that piqued his curiosity. With all his might, he pried up the lid and first spotted a few jugs of water. Without wasting a moment, he grabbed one, yanked out a large chewed-up cork, and drank his fill as the water streamed down his face, neck, and chest. Chucking the empty container to one side, he saw something that looked familiar. "What! It can't be. This looks like *my* dagger. How can that be? Someone has made plans for me. Hmmm... and I thought Ordak somehow sent me here. I'll get Zoltan for this." He said as a smile took over his face. "It must be nice to be a sorcerer." With a smirk, he nodded his head and raised the blade high above. "I'm sure this will come in handy." He placed it next to him on the deck.

In the corner of the old box, he saw a red silk scarf that covered a large round object. With the nimble hand of a magician, he yanked off the covering, and there rested a large orb of some kind. It appeared to be a good-sized melon. Puzzled, he reached for it, not knowing what to expect. First, with one finger, he poked it and discovered it was firm. Then, he slowly rubbed it with his other hand and sensed its warm, smooth surface. With both hands, he plucked it from its refuge. Somewhat heavy, he held it close to his ear, trying to detect any rumblings coming from within. He heard nothing.

"It's too large and light for a cannonball from an old ship...I don't think it's man-made... Hmmm..."

Elias balanced it in the palm of one hand and tapped on it with his fingernail. With his knuckle, he thumped on its smooth, curved surface. "Huh, I don't know what this could be." He shrugged his shoulders and gently placed it at his feet, and then he resumed rummaging through the oversized box.

A small, leather-bound book caught his eye. "Wow! What could this be?" He pulled it out, and the stained cover showed cracks due to years of sun, wind, and water. He couldn't make out a faded image that ornamented both the front and back. "What could this be?" He opened it. On the inside cover, he read the name Captain James Killybegs. "A captain's journal—how cool is that?" He began thumbing through the yellowed and stained pages and found an entry, a map of an island, and pages of notes that appeared to be gibberish. He was intrigued. "The Isle of Eahta. Hmmm, I wonder where that is," he said as he popped up his head and stretched his neck, looking in all directions. He saw no more than he did earlier—only the gray fog and the sun as it rolled in and out of some billowy, thick clouds. Looking back at the script, he read aloud:

"Monday, July 7, 1677. Only three crew and I survived the tumult. The Amaranthine and all aboard her were in search of the Elixir of Life, which lore proclaimed possessed great powers and would fetch a handsome penny. The day was clear, and what was our seventy-second day into the voyage when suddenly and without warning, She was engulfed in a veil of thick fog. Persisting for hours, I commanded to set anchor. As my crew attempted to carry out my order, The Amaranthine struck the land of an uncharted body. We later discovered the body was named Eahta—it was the Isle of Eahta.

The inhabitants of Eahta, many peculiar beings, graciously aided my crew to repair a gash to her bow. As the repairs commenced, I led a delegation to find the potion as this was, indeed, the isle of the celebrated Elixir. I marveled, as did the crew, of our turn of fortune—or so we thought.

Although I thought it was our third day on land, I was to find out it was, in all actuality, our seventh day on land when we found the elusive Elixir. It was guarded by a priestess in an exotic Temple. It took some doing to get there, but we forced a way through unfamiliar terrain. We battled creatures, beasts, and monsters as we approached the Temple. Misfortune came to all others in my delegation, but no harm came to me. I was the last man standing by the time I reached the treasure. The priestess was like no other woman I had ever seen. Her brown skin was adorned with colorful tattoos. She had the most unique sound to her voice—as if she was singing. A door to a special chamber was open. Her focus was elsewhere, and she was unaware of my presence. Having left the chamber unattended, and without her notice of me, or so I thought, I entered the room, took the goblet, and filled it with the Elixir, but the ground rumbled and violently shook for minutes. In some places, the earth opened, and scores of my crew were lost. I was to learn. Before the quake subsided, this holy woman, without spilling as much as a drop, pulled the cup from my grasp and swigged it whole. She said to me, "I am saving you from your own demise. Now be gone. Quickly."

Without the treasure, I fled. Once again, the fury of the isle unfurled as I hastened to make it to the safety of The Amaranthine, but from the shore, She was not to be seen. The last few members of my crew said they witnessed it being swallowed, sales and all, by a whirlpool in the blink of an eye. My first mate, Horace Greig, held on to a large sphere and claimed it was the real treasure. Knowing he had gone mad, my attention was on a lone lifeboat floating aimlessly near the shore. As we climbed aboard, the last seven of my compatriots and I found our way to the safety of the dark waves. I write this as the spray of the sea is becoming thicker, and Horace, now peering through a telescope, is warning me that a sea serpent is careening toward us.

Elias furiously flipped the pages, and there was nothing more written. "WHAT?" Elias barked out. "Where's the rest of it?" Elias leaned back against the wall of the boat. "Unbelievable! Just unbelievable. A sea serpent." He sat up, and his eyes bulged as he looked in all directions. He sat back and looked at the orb. "Hmmm, that's a treasure?"

Just then, something banged against the outer wall of the boat. *THWACK!* Surprised, Elias shot up, looked out, and examined the momentary calm waves all around him. *THWACK, THWACK!* He heard the booming noise coming from the opposite side of where he stood.

Abruptly, the craft began to teeter back and forth, and Elias had trouble with his footing. Stretching out his arms for balance was no use as the swaying became more violent, and the force of the intruder playing with the vessel frantically flung Elias to the deck. He hit the deck hard, but he quickly composed himself. Spotting the long oar, he reached for it and pulled himself up on two feet. Holding one end of the long pole as tight as he could with both hands, he thrust one end into the dark surface of the water, jabbing blindly, hoping to disturb whatever was causing the havoc. He continued to plunge the end of the oar, desperately trying to deter the invader. Unexpectedly, the phantom forcefully latched on to the oar and tugged on it, nearly pulling Elias overboard. When he jerked up on the long wooden pole, only half of it was there as something had bitten it off in two. "Well, now I'm really up the creek without a paddle," he said aloud, trying all he could to keep from an all-out panic.

Still having not laid an eye on his aggressor, Elias was unsure of what his next move should be. Just as the unwanted visitor arrived and rattled Elias' calm, now all was frightfully still—and quiet. The sea was tranquil, with only a pond like ripple here and there. Only seconds later, the intruder slowly began to pitch the boat back and forth. Much like a seesaw, the bow went up and then the stern. Each rocking motion began increasing with more force than the previous one, and the thrusting motion was more than Elias could handle. It sent him backward, catapulting him against the rough deck. He looked over his right shoulder, and there, emerging from the gray and ghastly depths surfaced an eel or snakelike creature with the diameter of an old oak tree back home. On the end of the gigantic, long body sat a gargantuan bony head of a dragon. It had a long snout laden with jagged horns. With a sort of sinister grin, it showed its long, spiked teeth. Before Elias could react, its slender tongue darted out of its mouth, and it let out a piercing shriek that sent a cold quiver down Elias' back. With an abrupt but fluid and graceful motion, the creature slipped beneath the surface, and all became still—again. This time, the unexpected calm and quiet seemed to last. As each second passed, Elias' tense muscles began to ease. Open-mouthed, he peered in all directions as sweat dripped down his cheeks.

Catching his breath, he said, "How weird was that? Maybe that *thing* is ..." Interrupted at that moment, the sea serpent, with a jerk, raised the bow skyward, rocketing most of the contents of the vessel to the stern, including Elias flipping end over end—all except the dagger that caught itself under a bench as almost everything plummeted toward Elias. White knuckled, Elias held on to a flimsy leg of a wooden bench. Catching a glimpse of the weapon, he could only shake his head in disappointment, as it was too far to reach. With no warning, the bow crashed to the surface of the water, and the force propelled Elias like a rag doll to the bow, where he landed spread eagle only inches from the gleaming dagger. The large ball he uncovered earlier rolled up between his legs. Like a flash of light, Elias said, "Ah-ha! I know what this is! That's all she wants—I hope."

He jumped to his feet and grabbed the egg. All was serene as he turned pensively and deliberately to survey the area. Too quiet, he thought, and with that, the creature surfaced, letting out another long, penetrating shriek. It wildly whipped its head back and forth, spewing and flicking streams of water like a dog after its bath. Standing tall, Elias held up the egg, and the creature suddenly became very still. The creature gently leaned its long body toward Elias. He heard its breath, and he thought that it didn't sound so different from his own. The serpent's large eyes stared at the egg, and then she turned her attention to Elias. He was moved as he looked into her eyes and no longer saw a fierce creature but saw a mother. Her eyes were warm. He nodded to her and motioned he was going to gently toss her the egg. She moved back, and he, with ease, lobbed the egg high into the air toward the mother. Her long tail cut through the water, and like a catcher's mitt, she caught the perfectly launched throw. She plunged into the water, and within a moment, she propelled herself from the trappings of the sea and was airborne, gliding above the boat only a few meters overhead. Elias could see just how mammoth and powerful she truly was. He felt a glow come from inside to out, and the corners of his lips turned up. Re-entering the water, she didn't resurface. This time, she was gone.

2
Hibush's Search for Power

Left for dead, Ordak lay squarely on his back on the rocky orange soil in the Forsaken Sea. The remote and most desolate place where Ordak, himself, banished his enemies over time during his evil reign. He was down a ravine where the Anthophiles—the Bee People—hid him from plain view to deteriorate into the filth of the Under World. He moaned as the pain and the poison from more than one hundred long sharp stingers protruded from his already grotesque but now deformed and swollen body. The acidic dust sat in the corners of his eyes and mouth as his body was awash with an orange tinge that covered everything in this barren land. The brilliance of the sun shone bright, and the heat and scorching rays only added to his tortured and lifeless body.

Many enormous, monstrous vulture-like birds lingered patiently gliding above in an elliptical pattern, keeping their tiny piercing eyes fixed on the comatose Ordak. Minuscule pests, some with many legs and pincers moving furiously, emerged from the slightest cracks in the ground and crawled on his flesh. Due to the venom and his weakened state, he could not summon the most basic movement, much less activate the most elementary dark power of his once great and evil arsenal to help himself. He was wasting away to oblivion.

♦ ♦ ♦

Once known as *The Conveyor of all Evil*, Ordak ruled the Kingdom of Gold, where he and the inhabitants lived in riches. The Kingdom was exquisite. Craftsmen from long ago carefully carved beautiful stones and gilded them in gold by order from Ordak. Tall stone towers, ornate sculptures, and stunning common areas abounded. Those chosen to live within the walls of the Kingdom, Ordak had called *Inhabitants*. Their homes were elegant and dripped with gold leaf. Ordak even instructed his workers to pave the streets in gold. Everything one could think of was made of or contained this precious metal.

Generations of Trolls quarried large gold rocks, much of it coming from the Seraph Region for the new Kingdom. With Ordak's expansion, he pushed the Seraphs farther and farther away to an area that he renamed the Seraph Region. Of all the creatures in the Under World, they are the most trustworthy. In the Under World, all knew that they were the last of the souls who sought good. As a people, they attempted to restore a balance. Although not yet achieved, this peaceful group stayed in the Under World to try to make a difference for all beasts and creatures, including Trolls, Ghouls, Pixies, Sarkanies, Minotaurs, and all the monstrous beings that dwelt there. The Seraphs knew that what first happened in the Under World found ways to emerge in the Middle World, where Elias came from. The Seraphs knew much rode on their shoulders.

In an earlier time that the Seraphs called The Great Domination of Ordak, Ordak had demanded them to join him to build a Kingdom that would be beyond reproach, and if they met his demand, he would reward the Seraph people. As irony would have it, Ordak deemed himself the architect of all that was beautiful. It was only when his overbearing pressure didn't lead to the results he wanted he disguised his ways and presented the Seraphs with an invitation to live in peace. Living in peace would be their way of life, with or without Ordak's interference. That 'peace,' according to Ordak, would come with only one rule. That rule was to pay homage to Ordak. It was then that the Seraphs walked away from

Ordak, but before they did, they demanded a treaty. Reluctant to do so, he agreed to a treaty that stands to this day. The agreement stated that Ordak would leave the Seraph people alone to live only in the Seraph Region.

Although the Seraph community was open to all, oddly, very few others in the Under World wanted their way of life. Riches and beauty were much more alluring. So, as it happened, beings of all kinds, whether they be gruesome, fiendish, or merely broken and misguided creatures, sought sanctuary by traveling to and living in the Kingdom of Gold. Material riches and beauty held a trance-like power over many in the Under World.

Those who followed Ordak were given the ability to transfigure, as all who lived there had to possess an outward beauty. Ordak issued a directive and decreed that every Inhabitant in public must take on a 'beautiful exterior.' Because he wanted the Kingdom to maintain the 'look' he wanted, the only punishment Ordak would impose for those who would not comply was banishment to the Forsaken Sea. Or sometimes—death. That was usually one and the same. The Inhabitants were forced to bow to Ordak and revere him. His authoritative rule was harsh and evil. This was the case until Elias disrupted Ordak's evil ways.

"Keep moving, you worthless Minotaur!" spouted Hibush. He rode in comfort in a carriage behind the massive Minotaur that he shackled at the ankles with only enough slack, allowing him to make sufficient strides to pull the Pixie. Bright red blood dripped from the beast's ankles as the sharp metal cuffs dug into his soft flesh. He grimaced on occasion, but this was not the way of the mighty Minotaur. Pewton walked to the side of Hibush, catering to all of his needs. Being a Troll, he was accustomed to serving others, knowing there was little chance he would ever have a break for a better life. When Ordak ruled, he reinforced the lowly life of Trolls. Nevertheless, Pewton sympathized with the Minotaur.

"Shouldn't we rest a moment or, perhaps two, master Hibush? The beast needs tending to."

"What do you care? I certainly don't." barked Hibush. "It's a bit jarring to hear you say that, Pewton. Where did your *compassion* come from? Certainly not from the Under World, where it is frowned upon—unless you're a Seraph. You're not one of *those*, are you?"

"I'm nothing but a Troll." Pewton shrugged his shoulders and looked away.

"Just as a reminder, I'm in control of the situation. I am the one with the power—am I not? The beast or Minotaur, whatever he is, is just fine. Look at him. He's a fine specimen of virility and, as such, needs no coddling from you, me, or anyone else." Blugwan rolled his eyes.

"Master," the Minotaur said with undetected sarcasm, "You may call me Blugwan."

"Why in the *Under World* would I stoop to your level and call you by *your* name?" Hibush said as if he took a waft of a sewer on a hot day. "After all, you betrayed Ordak and assisted Elias and his band of dissenters in destroying The Kingdom of Gold and setting the Inhabitants free. Did you not?"

Blugwan scowled but said nothing and kept pulling the carriage.

The sun was growing in intensity, and the rocky path and ill-fated conversation made it more unbearable for both Blugwan and Pewton. Hibush droned on.

"Everyone had what they wanted—all the gold they needed and the riches of what it could provide. All of them, beautiful...every last one. Look at me. I am now a tall, strong man that is the envy of all."

Undetected to Hibush, Blugwan and Pewton looked at the other with raised brows.

"Mastering transfiguration would do you both some good...oh, I forgot, the likes of you can be nothing but who you are. Huh. I, however, have digressed. Where was I? Oh yes—now, the Inhabitants of the Kingdom have nothing and look ordinary like their true selves. They are hideous at best. That pesky little Elias ruined it for all."

Blugwan cleared his throat and couldn't resist answering, "With all due respect, the Inhabitants are now happy and are making choices for their own futures, both pretty and ugly."

"What do you know? You're a dumb Minotaur—quite ugly, too," Hibush said as Pewton looked up with his bottom lip pushed out. Blugwan kept his calm.

Nervous, Pewton spoke. "Why Hibush—ah, ah master—without Elias, you would still be a mere Pixie working in the goldsmith's shop and under the, ah, ah, rule of Ordak."

Blugwan burst into an uncontrollable guffaw. Before Hibush could speak up, Blugwan said, "So, I understand that a certain Pixie—*you*—betrayed Gaspar, the goldsmith, and tricked Ordak, and now Ordak, who we're scouring the terrain for, is being picked apart by vultures."

"Shut up! You are both wrong!"

Blugwan wouldn't let it go. "Oh yes, I am sure he will be very happy to see you again. Or is that why you have a new appearance? Is the Pixie afraid? Huh?" Blugwan's hearty laughter echoed from the barren and rocky cliffs.

"SHUT UP! I will have no more of your insolence. We live in a world of betrayal. That's how I get my power. Without power, we have nothing. That's the way to get ahead—everyone knows that. I can't be faulted for coming up with a superior strategy to his. Ordak is such a fool...all that luscious power has gone to waste. The *evil one* let his guard down, and it was those—those irksome little *Bee* People who discarded him in this wasteland, not me."

"If this is what you say, master," Pewton said.

Hibush ignored him and continued, "His fabulous poison will ooze from his pores and evaporate into the universe unless we find him very soon so I can mop up what I can for my very own."

Hibush stopped there, and all that could be heard was the creaking of the carriage wheels and Blugwan's husky breath as he used his strength to pull Hibush along. Needing to hear himself orate, Hibush resumed.

"It matters not, *Minotaur*, if Ordak is *happy* to see me or not. His control over his own powers has all but vanished, I'm sure, and you, my friend, should be careful with what you say. I told you I'd let you go once we find him, but at this rate, I may change my mind."

"Yes sir—yes sir." Blugwan forced his answer and told him what he wanted to hear.

Pewton's heart sank to his stomach, and he felt confused and nervous. Seeing the chance to move forward in Hibush's eyes, he chimed in. "I, for one, do not want to be set free, sir, but want to help you. Pewton wants to be *your* servant."

"Very nice, Pewton, very nice. Blugwan, you can learn a great deal from the lowly Troll."

"Yes sir, I certainly can," Blugwan said softly and gave Pewton a stern look.

They pressed on in silence as the putrid and arid dust kicked up, leaving a pall behind them. Their death march persisted for hours.

3
Nattymama and Zoltan's Secret Plan

She kept her eyes tightly closed with her hands, palms up and open as they rested on her arthritic knees. There, she sat on the old stone bench as she often did at this time of day. Elias' grandmother, Nattymama, kept her thoughts streaming in her head as the sounds of the bubbling water cascaded from stone to stone in the small meandering brook only a few paces to her front.

All that separated her and her home was her sprawling circular herb garden that orbited a large sundial in its very center. All in her life intertwined with all around her and more. Most of what she needed or wanted was tucked off the rocky road on her modest parcel of land not far from where Elias grew up.

Her home had many windows and doors facing every direction. The hexagon-shaped bungalow teemed with books and artifacts from another time and place. Dried herbs hung from the dark beams above, and glass jars, ceramic containers, and an assortment of utensils, tools, and other paraphernalia adorned the many shelves and counters that filled her space. The most striking feature, constructed in the very center of her home, was a large, circular stone chimney with several fiery openings. Oftentimes, the staccato glow from the blaze within danced wildly against the walls of her home.

She sat motionless as the cool air filtered through each leaf, stem, and sprig of her garden. She detected a variety of scents and fragrances that made her senses come alive. The sun was warm that day, and on occasion, she lifted and tilted her head to face the rays coming from so far away. She was amazed that each distant ray created life in her and was all within arms' reach of her. Prayerfully and in a whisper, she would utter a word of gratitude.

Startled but not flinching one iota, she heard a muffled sound that came from her home. Her eyebrow pointed upward, and her chin poked forward. Then, all was calm as before, and she relaxed and reached back into her meditative state. No more than a moment later, she heard more ruckus coming from her bungalow. Eyes still closed, she tilted her head back and forth as if that might help her understand what she was experiencing. Slowly, she opened her eyes, scowled, and shook her head in exasperation.

"Mister Man—that cat. Must be. Why do I allow such creatures to rule my life? I will never know...probably got his tail caught in the door again," she said to herself. "Serves him right. Well, I need to take care of a potion or two anyway, so I best be getting up there before he does something stupid."

Not showing much urgency, she slowly stood and rubbed her palms together as she peered off to the peaks in the horizon. She inhaled the pure mountain air, only to be interrupted once more by the muffled sounds.

"All right already, I'm coming," she blurted. "That mangy cat is going to get the best of me one of these days."

She ambled up the slight hill and through her garden; she paused a moment and leaned over the ginkgo, pulled off a leaf, and held it to her nose. With her bottom lip pushing forward, she shook her head. "I don't know what's going on. Perhaps too many nasty weeds are keeping what is good from blossoming."

Now more acute to her ears, the muffled sound became sharper and stronger. *Bang, bang, bang!* "Oh goodness, let me get inside." She rushed into her sunlit home and scanned the premises. Perplexed, she scratched her head and began to walk slowly around the room, inspecting the cabinets and doors. "Where is that cat?" *Bang, bang, bang!* "Ah, that Mister Man has locked himself in that cabinet overhead," she said with conviction. "How in the world could he get in there? I always keep this one locked tight... uh! Ahhh, could it be that I have a guest?" She unlatched the door leading to an extra-large compartment, and before she had pulled the creaky door completely open, a voice came.

"Well, my dear, whatever took you so long?"

"Oh my—Zoltan!" said Nattymama. "Is it really you?"

"Yes, in the flesh...any longer, you would have found mere bones, my good lady...perhaps you can be a love and help me out of here. The fragrance of fairy wings is getting to me. It is quite a tight fit, and, you see, I would rather stand for a bit instead of lying here in the dark. I'm just a century or so too old for certain kinds of transportation."

"Of course...of course, but it isn't fairy wings you smell but barrenwort—there *IS* a difference, you know?" She reached out her hand, and when their fingers touched, they simultaneously looked into each other's eyes and then looked away—and then back with a smile.

"It has been a long time since we've seen one another," Zoltan said as he shimmied out of the dark space and stood before her. He brushed off the dust and combed his beard with his fingers. "There. I think I am all here now. And hopefully presentable."

"Please sit for a while. I'll pour you a cup of my special herb tea," she said and then looked at him. "My, how I've missed you, you old sorcerer."

"And I too...Yes, I think a cup of your special herbal tea sounds grand. The supply you gave me years ago has long gone dry, and how I've yearned for yet another sip. After all, one cannot live on only the black coffee I drink and the hard-boiled eggs I eat." Zoltan piped up.

"Coming right up," Nattymama said, looking him over. "My, it has been a very long time...oh, yes, the tea," she said, going one direction and pivoting to go another.

Nattymama began clanging pots and utensils together as she searched for just the right mug. She placed a battered iron kettle on the red-hot coals of her circular brick stove. Zoltan watched her every move with delight and offered a quick, lopsided grin.

"So, dear Nattymama, I assume you are wondering why I was in your cabinet."

Without so much as skipping a beat, she said, "Yes, I was wondering that. Indeed I was, but I knew you were going to tell me sooner or later." She paused and then continued, "I am assuming that Elias and the others are on their way as well." She looked back to the cabinet.

Zoltan cleared his throat and said, "Well, first of all, I was very pleased that I remembered that you have an active portal. I had to act as fast as a spark glowing bright and then disappearing. It was your face that came to mind."

She looked up and walked slowly to Zoltan and said, "Why yes, the portal is quite active, and no one, other than you, knows about it...so are we expecting Elias any moment?" she said, walking over to the cabinet opening and then peering inside.

"That's what we must talk about."

Nattymama turned quietly and faced Zoltan. She walked over to the table where he was sitting and sat across from him, paused, and then blurted at the top of her lungs, "You left my dear Elias?"

"I didn't exactly leave the boy. Things have a way of changing in the Under World. You know how that is?" he asked, looking away from her.

"I do, Zoltan, but the rainbow spell was foolproof. That portal was the strongest I have ever made and the prettiest, I might add."

"Yes, the rainbow was quite beautiful...but the boy has the gift. You know that. And I had no choice in the matter as I saw it."

"You had 'no choice' in what matter?" said Nattymama as her eye twitched.

"Perhaps I should tell you first that our clever Elias used the powers of the Endless Within to seize the Kingdom of Gold...I must hand it to Tas. He is one good mystic. Yes, *he* is. I believe Elias' journey to study his ways was *your* brilliant idea, was it not?" Zoltan asked as he looked away and nervously twiddled his thumbs.

"Go on, go on. Tell me more," Giving him no wiggle room, Nattymama leaned toward Zoltan.

"Oh, yes. Elias pointed his dagger to the sky with one hand and touched the amulet with the other. He uttered the command, and a blinding, colorful beam shot from the tip of the blade to the blue sky. What was next was nothing but spectacular—it was brilliant."

"Yes, yes. Go ahead." Nattymama folded her arms against her chest.

"A jagged bolt of lightning blasted from the clear sky and touched down on the orange and red soil nearby. Thick black clouds rumbled and rolled in from nowhere and built upon each other in the sky like layers of lava. The zigzag of lightning bolts burst and exploded from high in the heavens to the crusty lifeless surface."

"Ah, I think I know where this is going," like ice melting, a gleeful Nattymama smiled.

"The surface of the rocky ground began fuming yellow and red gas."

"Oh, I most definitely know where this is headed," she said, still smiling.

"A few drops of rain began to fall from the new clouds. The next thing you know, more rain fell, and a ripe tang of electricity dripped from the air."

"How marvelous, he used lightning—very nice, very nice indeed," Nattymama said as she clapped her hands a few times.

"Yes, he did. But would you like to know why?" Zoltan asked proudly.

"I already know, but go on...you tell me."

"He used Aqua Regia," Zoltan said.

"Yes, yes. I knew that. It is Royal Water and is the only substance that can corrode gold. Doesn't destroy it, but its fury is sure to melt it, and it seeps in every pore and crevasse below."

"Yes, my dear—you are correct," Zoltan added.

"My, my. He drenched the Kingdom of Gold with nitric-hydrochloric acid. Clever, clever boy," she said, beaming. "But Zoltan, why did you divert him from coming home? Didn't he defeat the Dark Warrior—the evil one?"

Zoltan sat up straight, reached for his beard, and looked directly at Nattymama. "I sensed something was deadly wrong amid the mayhem. I conjured up a power that I have rarely used, and honestly, I surprised myself that I could still tap into a darker vibration."

"Goodness, Zoltan. Dark powers can sometimes rebound and must be used only as a last resort."

"You are absolutely correct, my dear woman. However, at my advanced age, my time is running out, and although I was very uncomfortable doing so, I had to risk it," he said as his forehead wrinkled. "Anyway, moments before the goldsmith shop was engulfed in flames, I was able to read these cosmic stirs or rhythms. I was able to read the smoke that came from the ghastly destruction."

"Ah...of course, you used the ancient art of *smoke reading* that I nearly forgot about...hmmm. Yes, it is very dark magic...so what else? Tell me. Don't keep me hanging, you old wizard."

"I must admit, I am a tad rusty reading something as dark as the telepathy that sprouts from evil, but I was able to discern that Hibush, the menacing Pixie, was able to hoodwink Ordak one more time."

"Pixies! They are among the worst of all the fraudsters in the Under World. They are far from what they seem. Please tell me more."

"What I determined was that Hibush said he had studied the Dark Warrior, that he had devoured the knowledge he needed to conquer eternity, and that he planned to go somewhere that he would become invincible to reign supreme. And with that, he bid Ordak a farewell and vanished before Ordak could react. As if there was not enough fire already, that's when Ordak set the place ablaze."

"*The Isle of Eahta.*" Nattymama blurted. "It's got to be Eahta."

"Yes, dear woman, my thoughts precisely. Elias is our best chance."

"Even if I didn't agree with you, you have already sent him there, yes?"

"As I said, Elias is our best chance," Zoltan said once more. "Elias will soar beyond his wildest expectations—and ours!"

Shaking her head, Nattymama stood and walked to the window, looked to the Mountain of Sirok, and said, "I would have acted in the same manner, you old magic maker." After a pause, she turned and quickly walked to a gigantic old sideboard and pulled open the second drawer. Pulling out papers, string, and other seemingly random items, the blur of her hands abruptly ceased. She found a large dusty book and began to thumb through the pages. She tore a page from the old tome and chanted a favorite spell she used around her bungalow, and the page folded itself up to not much larger than a postal stamp. "There. It fits anywhere. It's a convenient spell in such a cozy bungalow," she said with her hands on her hips and looking from side to side. "Hmmm, maybe I need to use it more often."

With her back to Zoltan, he scratched his head with his pinky. "And what, pray tell, are you doing?" Nattymama turned and faced Zoltan, holding up the folded page.

"We must get this to him."

"Nattymama, I will see to it. I will go at once. But what is it?"

"Never mind that. It is his ticket to find the truth."

"Rest assured, I will hand deliver it to the boy."

"Are you sure, Zoltan? Your place in all this is fading, I am sorry to say," said Nattymama.

"Fading? I wasn't quite ready to describe my relevance as *fading*. I have but one more service, well, two now, to render. I have a very important message to deliver to Elias as well."

"Ah, Zoltan, I am happy."

"This new adventure has given me a final purpose and has given me a newfound life."

"So you have finally decided to tell…"

"Yes, yes, I have. Those words shall not be uttered until the time has come."

With that, Nattymama handed him the tiny page. Zoltan held it by the tips of his long fingers as he tucked it into his pocket and said, "It is as light as the tip of a Turul feather. What is your message with this finely folded folio?

"You tell him that this is from his Nattymama."

"Yes—yes, go on."

"You tell him to find Shin—you remember him?"

"Oh, of course. He is a sorcerer of another kind. He is a master at finding the truth in all we do." Zoltan crooked his head and looked at the ceiling. "Sometimes I wish I would have gone that direction with my powers."

"No time to second guess yourself, Zoltan."

"*Ahem...*as usual, you are correct."

"Yes, and we must get back to the task at hand. Elias must present this page to Shin, and he will be able to help him find his way to the Temple. More specifically—the Elixir."

"You are so right, dear Nattymama."

"I am sure he will help Elias figure out the key to opening the chamber door before the gong sounds on the eighth day. He must go to the Temple and detract all others, whether it be Hibush or some other evil being. He must get there first." she said.

"That's it?"

"Heavens, yes. Any more than that, and it will be too much. He will know the circumstances when he is in the thick of things."

"Hmmm. Unwilling to tell me more, I will convey your message and this small, very neatly folded page—and I know, my dear, when not to ask for anymore."

"You are smarter than you look—and you look pretty smart. Besides, we do not have all the answers, but knowing the right questions to ask is most important. Answers will come if we do that," she said, and they both laughed. She continued and said, "If I tell you more, I risk unnaturally altering the cosmos—but you know that."

"Oh my...yes, tell me no more."

"You must go. Remember Zoltan, you must give him this so he may find Shin, or he will surely be doomed. The island is a mystery, and all who have tried to unravel its meaning have failed. But as a defender of the Elixir yourself, you know that from your younger days."

"That I do. And I certainly noticed you added the word 'younger.'"

Paying little attention to Zoltan's comments, she walked to the window and stared out. "He must go in with an open mind—and heart. He must follow the ways of the island and the Temple, as there are no shortcuts. Greedy and thoughtless men have tried to find the Elixir without taking it step by step. The consequences are great."

"Very well, my dear," Zoltan smiled and nodded. He patted his pocket. "I will get this to him." He then pulled a step stool over to the cabinet where Nattymama first found him and climbed upon it. Attempting to enter one way and then positioning himself another, Zoltan eventually managed to maneuver, feet first, into the small dark space. His head appeared at the opening. "I must say that I am ready to go, so if you please close the door, I will slip into the Under World once again." He paused. "This may be my final trip."

"Final-*schminal!*" Nattymama climbed onto the step stool, looked at Zoltan, and simply nodded. She placed her warm palm on his cheek and smiled. Maintaining eye contact, she slowly closed the door. "Goodbye, my Zoltan. It is with love I send you off." Turning her head and moving her ear close to the door, she heard nothing. She put her fingers to her lips and kissed them, then she touched the door and closed her eyes. A few seconds later, her face lit up with a smile as she opened her eyes.

"That's that," she said, wiping her hands on her apron. She stepped down, and as she did, something at her feet caught her attention. As her eyes focused, she realized what was underfoot. It was the folded page.

4
Failed Attempt

The relentless sun was blinding to the trio who trudged through the Under World in the Forsaken Sea in search of Ordak. The sky was white and appeared to have blotted blood stains throughout. Moving is silence except for the creaking wheels and an occasional caw from gigantic, bony birds with long beaks who anticipated their next meal.

"Look! Up ahead, Hibush—I think we've found your prize," shouted Blugwan.

"Pull this thing faster, you beast. Have you no regard for my well-being," Hibush said as he leaned forward and shielded his eyes from the glaring sun.

Looking back to Hibush, Blugwan jerked the cart as Hibush squealed with anger. "You are who you are because of who you are, you, you Minotaur."

"Yep," said Blugwan. "Did you mean to rhyme?"

"Ugh...you are insufferable."

In another minute or so, the three stood only a few paces from the limp and lifeless body of the Dark Warrior and the once Conveyor of All Evil.

"Look at him...pitiful," sneered Hibush. "To think that all in the Under World feared this pile of rubbish. All it took was the venom of a different sort to snuff him out. Little Bee People was all it took. Who would have ever thought?"

Blugwan wasn't ready to let that one slip by without a response. "Elias knew the Bee People would help,"

"Enough from you. Just a reminder, I have your fate in my hands. That's both of you."

The more Hibush spoke, the more Ordak woke from his semi-conscious state to one of awareness. His body, although, was still paralyzed by hundreds of slender points of poison. Mindful of his onlookers, Ordak kept his eyes closed but understood all that was going on around him. Hibush squatted next to Ordak and poked at his face with his index finger. "What a horrible way to go, but how glorious this is for me." He lifted Ordak's arm and dropped it, falling hard onto the rocky surface. He stood and kicked his leg—no reaction. He kicked him several times. "I rather like this," he said with a sick cackle.

Blugwan looked on with amazement as Pewton took a few paces backward. "What a disgusting Pixie," Blugwan whispered to Pewton.

"What? Did you say something, Minotaur?"

"No, I was merely clearing my throat from the disgust of this place. It gets in places, and it's hard to swallow."

"Oh, I see. I don't care anyway. Pewton—Blugwan, this was your master. Think of that. This was the Warrior of Darkness who toyed with every soul in his wake like a puppeteer. He was the..."

"...ah, ah Hibush—I mean, sir, you said once you found Ordak, you would set me free," Blugwan said as he tugged on the chains.

Upon hearing the name Hibush, Ordak opened his eyes for a moment.

Answering Blugwan, Hibush said, "You interrupted me, you beast!" He paused and shook his head in disgust. "Yes, I know I promised you freedom. What is your hurry?"

"Sir," Pewton piped up, "I will serve you even if the Minotaur deserts you."

Blugwan snarled and said, "I will never figure out you Trolls."

"Very good of you, Troll—very good. Although you disgust me, I will find use for you in my empire. Thank you for reminding me of your so-called loyalty."

"That's why we came here? To anoint you Ordak's successor? I knew you wanted his powers but missed the part where you wanted to be the next terror in the Under World," said Blugwan.

"Nicely put...yes, that's precisely what I am going to do. I needed a brute like you to provide my transportation, and I needed a servant. Why do you think you're in chains?"

"I'm in chains because what magic you do possess, you used against us and imprisoned me and the Troll."

"Say what you want, but I needed the strength of a Minotaur and someone wishy-washy like Pewton. Let me put it this way. The Troll is submissive, and you are the lucky Minotaur. Besides, it's temporary."

Blugwan felt the blood rush to his head. He tightened his stare on Hibush as his nostrils flared. He grumbled but kept his anger at bay.

"Besides, I knew you were both idiots and could not provide me with competition or worry. As I see it, neither of you has anything worth salvaging after this long slog anyway. If you have any in you, the evil in you is garden variety, nothing more—perhaps you are even 'good' and how disgusting that prospect is. I am in no need of it. I am happy to free you, and if Pewton wishes to continue to serve me, so be it. You may go now...I told you that you are free," Hibush said.

Rattling the chains, Blugwan looked down at his feet.

"I suppose you want those off too?" Hibush asked with a few short shakes of his head; he pulled a key from his pocket and unlocked his shackles.

"I will go and take the Troll."

"Be my guest—take him if he'll go with you, but look at yourself, and you can give him nothing. How can he resist me and what I will become."

Massaging his wrists, Blugwan started walking away. "Pewton, are you coming with me?"

Blugwan stopped in his tracks as his eyes widened. He turned to face Hibush and Pewton. He drew in a large audible breath. Pewton looked back at Hibush, and he shook his head and moved closer to him. Hibush grinned and let out a short burst of laughter, then placed his fingers over his mouth.

"Have it your way." Blugwan was gone within seconds. He walked about one hundred paces away and behind some large boulders. He was clearly out of sight when he paused and turned back. Being as quiet as a huge Minotaur could be, he circled back around and cautiously climbed a rocky hill on the opposite side to where the other three were. High above them on a massive cliff, he found refuge in an alcove hidden from sight, but he was able to clearly see and hear the goings-on of the small but evil enclave.

Although transfigured, Hibush maintained his large and sensitive ears, and they perked up. His eyes shot back and forth.

"Did you hear that?"

"Pewton heard nothing, master."

"Funny, but I am rarely wrong on such matters," said Hibush.

Rumblings to one side gave way to a few boulders that plummeted to the ground where they stood. Their heads snapped upwards, and they saw the vulture perched where the rocks once were.

"Get out of here, you long-necked, redheaded scavengers!" Hibush screamed. The vultures held their ground. Not being able to scatter the nuisances, he settled himself down and looked at Pewton with arrogance as if he were the victor.

"Enough of that. Let's get down to business. Pewton, you step aside and give me room."

"Yes, master, but how will you gain so much power from someone so weak?"

"Stupid, stupid little Troll. I wouldn't expect you to understand. He has all his evil ways, but his power is inert. Inert! It's there but inactive. I will sever his power from him as he severed the power from all the lowly creatures he devoured."

"Devoured?"

"Let me put it this way. I have learned Ordak's secret. I studied his every move and acquired his ways of wrenching every ounce of evil force from the victims he ensnared, thus endowing himself with inconceivable malevolent power. It is so sickly wicked; it's beautiful."

"Beautiful? So...so...so," Pewton stammered.

"Spit it out," Hibush said as he paced and waved his arms to punctuate his description.

"How will you gain his power?"

"Simple. Me and my 'big' ears spent hours roaming his castle—no one knew. I found a room that was sealed off. Being 'sealed off' was my first clue. Clever as I am, it wasn't long before I was in the vault. It was full of ancient books and manuscripts. I knew there was something in all those yellowed pages that was off-limits to all those in the Kingdom, so I read every last word. After some time, being the patient Pixie I am, I found the

31

book with the very sentence of the enchantment that extracts his dark powers and transfers them, one by one, into someone else. That someone else will be me."

"I see," Pewton said with a grin as he perked up.

"Ah, you think I'm an idiot. You will never hear me utter one syllable of that spell in your presence. I have ways so that you will know nothing. But you interrupted me. Where was I? Oh yes, I will then yank the ring off his finger on his left hand and place it on my finger. With the words he kept secret and his ring of evil, I will twist and wring his vile and corrupted powers from him and fill myself with all he has. These same powers he has collected over the centuries will pour out and become one with me."

"Please excuse Pewton, but...but you said yourself, it only took the 'nectar' of a hundred swarming Bee People to render him paralyzed. I beg of you, master, leave the body to rot and allow the vultures a treat. Let his venom dilute itself into the cosmos. I beg of you to do something else, like, like...."

"...let me fill in the blank for you – 'good?' You want me to do something else like being 'good.' I will leave that for Elias, but see, he is gone—he is far away from here. By now, he should be comfortably in the Middle World dabbling with a paintbrush or doing chores on the farm—all that stuff the mortals do in the Middle World.

"Why master, why?"

Paying no attention to Pewton, the veins in Hibush's neck protruded, his eyes bulged, and his body stiff and cold. "I, on the other hand, will control the Under World, and in time, my hold and influence will sprout from the cracks to the Middle World, but by that time, it will be too late for Elias or any other *hero wannabes,* to counteract what I put in motion as I will be unstoppable."

"Now that those of the Under World know how Ordak was defeated, you do not stand a chance—I say that, of course, with the utmost respect, master," Pewton said as his shoulders hung low and his eyes gazed down to the pebbles on the ground.

"You are such a dimwit that you sound almost intelligent. I'll put it this way if you must know, and I think I am safe telling you such things with Elias safely gone. I now will have easy access to travel from here to the Temple on the Isle of Eahta and sip from the cup. With my accumulation of evil and the *contents* of *that* cup, my reign will never end. I will control life. That, my friend, is something Ordak NEVER accomplished. That's the missing piece. I will be the evilest force in the cosmos, and my power will go unmatched."

"Master, forgive me, but what then? Why must you do this?"

"What are you talking about? Do what?" Hibush asked, flailing his arms as he grew more agitated with each breath. His piercing eyes went right through Pewton.

Now terrified, Pewton began slowly backing away. "Ah...ah...I mean...why must you use your powers to..."

Before Pewton could summon his next words, Hibush raised his hand and pointed his spindly fingers at the Troll. From each finger, he sent narrow beams of power that pounded Pewton in the chest and sent him back many paces, and his eyes rolled back into his head.

"Sorry, Pewton, what was it you were trying to ask me? Was it: will I use my powers to wipe out the likes of you? If so, yes." With that, he sent another narrow beam from his finger toward Pewton, and this time, he was left paralyzed and appeared near death.

The whole event was too sudden for Blugwan to react from his hidden sanctuary. He bit his tongue as his blood raced through his large, hammering heart. "Hibush will not get away with this," he whispered.

Hibush looked to where Blugwan sat as the Minotaur crouched deeper into the alcove. Ordak began to twitch his leg and to clench and release his fist, but this was all undetected by Hibush. Blugwan, however, noticed his movements immediately. He leaned forward and tightened his focus on Ordak. With his thumb, Ordak turned his ring on his finger several times. Then Ordak was again completely still.

"Ordak," Hibush said, looking down at his prey, "Your day has come to an end. You let the boy destroy you. You, the mighty Conveyor of All Evil—the Dark Warrior—the fool! That's all you were—a fool," Hibush cackled and then continued. "You wanted a kingdom, and you played to the Inhabitants' narcissistic tendencies, giving them beauty and wealth and asking them in return to obey and bow down to you. But a little boy disrupted your plan. A *little* boy." He paused and looked out to the barren landscape. "Well, I want more than a kingdom. I will not give *them* ANYTHING! I want more. I deserve more. I want the universe!"

"The universe?" Ordak said with a strong and full-throated response.

"You are...you're CON-CONSCIOUS?" Hibush stuttered.

"I am emerging like a hibernating beast, and my powers are mutating to that of an even more insidious evil. Something you cannot understand as you sound like an unschooled imitator and not like a powerful ruler. You know nothing of my powers," Ordak said, still barely able to move.

"You...you are wrong. You are tricking me—I don't believe you. Yes, that's what you are doing." Hibush backed away. He raised his hand and pointed to Ordak. He sent the most powerful force he knew directly at Ordak. To Hibush's shock, the high-intensity beam of energy was redirected to Ordak's ring.

"My warning to you, Hibush, your newly acquired powers are simple at best, as you can see. Now, just like that, I have them. But the secret is much more than the powers. The only way to grow absolute power is to gather allies who you may eventually mold without them even knowing of their own transformation. Tell them what they want to hear. Give them hope for something better. It's called being the master of deception. You just let the Minitour free, and the Troll is nearly dead. Even evil cannot be evil alone. I have one more thing to tell you."

"Ah, ah, what is it?"

Ordak lifted himself from the rocky ground and now stood in front of Hibush. With a twisted smile, he winked at him and raised his arm, showing him the ring. It sparkled in the sunlight. "You plan to take this ring, the malevolent opposite of Zoltan's ring, for 'good,' and then plan to travel to the Isle of Eahta to sip the Elixir?"

"Perhaps." Hibush crossed his arms and poked out his chin.

"I heard you say so." Ordak straightened his crooked spine the best he could and hissed.

"Yes then—you fool. YES." Hibush looked Ordak in the eyes and said nothing more.

Ordak laughed. "You're still calling me a 'fool.' How remarkable of you. But my question is, how do you plan to get there?"

"Look at you. You can barely stand. You are in no position to question me." Hibush found his nerve and stepped closer to Ordak.

"You are a very funny Pixie. Have you forgotten what just took place? Besides, we are surrounded by thousands of miles of bleak desert, and Eahta is an island. A little island surrounded by water. It lives in a parallel dimension. Now that you have decided to do this alone, my question stands. Once you do away with me, how do you plan to get there? Do you know the spell that opens a portal?"

"Ah, ah, of course I do." Hibush stammered and flailed his arms as he spoke.

"Ha! I don't think you do, Pixie."

Hibush stood frozen as he thought through Ordak's logic. "I will, I will, I will find the portal. I will finish my task with you and suck the powers you possess and will find my way to Eahta. Hibush paused and continued with newfound confidence. "After all, I know the enchantment that will yank the dark forces of evil from every fiber of your decerped being."

"Pitiful. You actually think you have learned my evil ways, but you must have missed the class on my regenerative energies. See, since you arrived, I have pulled from you every ounce of *your* powers and claimed them for myself. Not just the meager powers you just used to try to subdue me. See, as once a smart and promising sorcerer, I have amassed a thousand years of dark and destructive magic."

"What? You lie! Look at you. You are a shriveled-up version of your evil self. Enough talk." Hibush began the enchantment, but before he could utter the second syllable, Ordak raised his arm, and through his fingers, he sent five lightning streams that sent Hibush through the air. Motionless, he lay beside Pewton, awaking Pewton, who began to stir.

Blugwan watched in awe. Ordak inhaled a deep breath and let out a loud, hideous screech. He extended both arms and waved them, saying, "The Isle of Eahta, the land of no time and the Elixir of Life. Thank you, Hibush. You were so right about one thing. I was thinking way too small. Thank you. I, too, want more than a kingdom." He turned and raised his left hand to the sky. His ring eerily glowed. With a boom, he bellowed, "OPEN PORTAL – APERI PORTAE AD AEHTA!"

From a speck of dust, colorful rings emerged and grew into a whirlwind. The colors were vivid, clear, and bold. Ordak turned and looked at Hibush and shook his head in delight. As a king would do, he raised his chin and processed into the portal. He vanished.

Blugwan rushed down from his hiding place and stood in front of the portal that was beginning to fade, and with no hesitation, he entered the circles. With one eye open, Pewton witnessed everything. He looked at Hibush, who was not moving. With all his might, he crawled toward the portal, and as he did, the colors became less intense and nearly vanished. Out of desperation, he pulled himself up and lunged into the portal, which was more of a fall. As he cleared the opening, any hint of color that was still hovering faded and then disappeared.

5
Climb The Stem

Weary from his encounter with the Sea Serpent, Elias stretched out squarely in the middle of the boat's deck. His thoughts wandered at best, but without notice, they pulled him back to some frightening moments. He, however, felt gratified for untangling the scary event and helping a mom. Images of her huge bony head that disagreed with her graceful cylindrical body were imprinted in his mind. Worst of all was her shriek, and he winced as he brought it to mind. What did it all mean? The serpent—the journal—his exile? Of all places, why was he here? While wondering where land could be hiding, the faces of his friends and family overpowered all his thoughts. All he could think was, *will he ever see them again?*

Restless, he fiddled with a thick, coarse rope coiled to one side as he looked to the sky. Drained by his rocky voyage, he remained listless on his back as he, biding time, picked up the dagger and examined it closely. Squinting, he focused on every scratch or nuance on the cold metal blade. He delicately touched the tip of his index finger on the tiny point, and as he did, he mouthed the sound 'ow' while his nose twisted up on one side. Still on his back, he grabbed the hilt with two hands, and with outstretched arms, he pointed it to the blur of the heavens, ruminating about his first night on Sirok. That's when he plucked a powerful sword from a secret vault told to him by Nattymama. The sword, he mused, saved his life on a couple of occasions when he skillfully severed the heads of the Sarkany—the three-headed, shape-shifting dragon. "Existo verus ut vestri," he whispered, followed by, "Be true to yourself. Think of that...that was written on the blade itself, and I didn't even know it at the time...can't complain, as it served me well, but this oversized pen knife has done right by me too."

WHOOSH. At that moment, jarring him from his comfort, he heard a gigantic splash only twenty paces or so from the bow of the boat. The wave it made jostled the little craft as he jumped to his feet. With a wrinkled brow and his jaw hanging low, he peered from side to side. Keeping one eye on the white-capped waves, he reached back to grab his dagger. Bubbles jetted to the surface of the choppy water, and he waited to see if anything would pop up. Only a second later, bobbing before him, the back of a man's head emerged, gasping uncontrollably for air. Ardently treading water, he turned, and Elias saw who thrashed about before him. He could barely believe his eyes.

"ZOLTAN. Is that really you?"

Zoltan, now exhausted but surprisingly calm, answered Elias. "It is I," he gasped. "...and I came *so very* close to landing on the dry planks... of your vessel...right beside you." Water splashed a few times in his face.

"...but...but I can't believe it," Elias said, reacting in amazement.

"Not to be rude, my boy, but I'm not interested in conversing at this point. Be a good man and put down your weapon to throw me a line to welcome me aboard."

"Oh yeah...sorry." With a cold slap, Elias was brought back to reality as he hurriedly tied one end of the rope to an iron ring attached to the floorboards of the deck and tossed the bulk of the looped hemp to Zoltan. He wrapped it around his arms, and like a vice, he held on securely with both hands. With somewhat of a struggle, like reeling in a blue marlin, Elias was able to tow Zoltan up and over the edge of the side of the boat. He delivered him safely to the dry deck of the lifeboat. Both Zoltan and Elias collapsed like a sack of potatoes.

"Zoltan, are you alright? What are you doing here? Why is..."

"Not all at once," Zoltan said, pulling himself up to a seated position, clearing his throat between words and poking his pinky finger in one ear. "I've come chasing you, Elias. I sent you here...do you have a blanket in there?" he asked, pointing to the large wooden box.

Elias froze. "Wait, what? You *sent* me here?" His jaw jutted forward, and he scowled at his guest.

Zoltan kindly smiled and exhaled. He shrugged his shoulders and joined his hands together in a prayerful fashion.

"I knew it. I don't know why I reacted so surprised. I knew something was up, especially since I found my dagger here, but...why?" Elias said, folding his arms against his chest.

"My good boy, I could see no other way. You have the gift, the donum...now the blanket, if you will." Zoltan stretched out his shivering hands.

"The donum...the DONUM...this gift is a curse! What else...what else can you tell me?" Elias retrieved a moldy moth-eaten blanket from the box and gently wrapped it around Zoltan's shoulders.

"If you settle yourself down one iota, I will tell you—you temperamental artists are something else," he kindheartedly said under his breath.

Elias' shoulders sank, and he let out a sigh as he sat next to the old man.

"I detected something sinister as the smoke of the kingdom wafted our way," Zoltan said with an easy monotone. Now for a cup of coffee. Do you have one?"

"What? Coffee? Are you serious? We're on a banged-up boat in the middle of nowhere. What are you thinking?"

"I see your point," Zoltan said as he placed his hands one over the other and quickly clapped his upper hand to his lower, at which time a hot pot of steaming coffee and two mugs hovered before them.

"Awesome, Zoltan. You'll have to teach me that one," Elias said as he briefly forgot about his frustration with his new and unasked-for adventure.

"Oh, you will learn how and quite a bit more. Now pour the coffee, and let's talk," said Zoltan as a soft, salty breeze gave him a slight stir.

Elias poured the coffee and looked with admiration at his old friend. "So what can you tell me?"

Using both hands to sip from the mug, Zoltan said, "I can tell you very little at this point. I have a morsel of information to share, but not much. Believe me when I say I know very little."

Short-fused, Elias blurted out, "A morsel. A morsel! You send me *here*, and YOU CAN'T TELL ME WHY?" You know I was just attacked by a sea serpent and..."

"Good for you, Elias," Zoltan interjected gleefully, cutting Elias off mid-sentence. "You must have fared quite well as I do not see any hideous blemishes on you, and I don't see the serpent anywhere," Zoltan added while looking out to the vast gray rolling waves.

Collecting his thoughts, Elias knew his frayed nerves would lead him somewhere he'd rather keep to himself and took a deep breath. "I'm sorry Zoltan...I'm tired and so... alone." Elias looked down at his hands, sniffed a few times, and then rubbed his nose. He looked out to the sea as a breeze caught his floppy hair and tousled it in a few directions. "Like I was abandoned until you showed up. I just don't know what to make of all this. It's time for me to go home and do what I want to do. I earned it, after all. That's why I traveled to find you in the first place—to find out who I am and do what I love. And traveling to the Under World to find you and all I did there. I've done enough—I've earned it."

"You earned it? Yes, I can see your point. First of all, thank you as you saved me from the clutches of Ordak, and you are quite humble as you set the oppressed folks of the kingdom free. But my good boy, I am sorry to say that, now, those things matter not, at least not for the short run."

"Huh? I feel my life is out of control."

"Elias, life is full of the unexpected, but we seem to forget that and think life SHOULD be full of the 'expected,' Zoltan said in a very calm but exacting tone. "You are in the middle of, shall I say, a twist and, for that matter, a turn—and perhaps another twist. I must say you are who you are whether you like it or not, and you should think of it as a privilege to be you and grab hold of every moment of your life. It is up to you to make the most of it. Let me pour you another cup of coffee."

"Okay, okay, but I don't like it, and I'm not talking about the coffee," Elias said, sitting back and looking at the sea. It was now quiet as the endless waves that relentlessly wrapped themselves around the boat seemed like a warm embrace as they continued to lap lower against the sides. It was still.

"I know you are unhappy with me, and you have every right to be so, but in the end, you will understand. You will. Trust me."

Ignoring Zoltan's words, Elias asked, "So tell me, how is everyone—Kelsa?"

"She is just fine. I managed to redirect both her and Cimbora safely to a place where you will see them soon. Don't ask me why, as I had to act quickly when Ordak was breathing down our necks—before our dear friends, the Bee People, whisked him away. Oh, that was such a special moment just hearing the hum." They both laughed and sipped from their cups.

"I think I know the moment—yeah, the exact moment. He almost picked up on what you were doing. I could tell you were doing something, but I had no clue," said Elias.

"To tell you the truth, I was not so sure myself." Zoltan winked.

"And the others?" Elias asked abruptly, changing the subject.

"Nattymama and your family are fine. Oh yes, and before I forget, you must understand that time counts differently there versus here. It may seem like only a minute to some but an eternity to others, but this will all be clearer to you later."

"You haven't even told me where I'm going."

"Oh yes. In a moment," Zoltan replied with a light chuckle. "As far as the others, Lantos and Gaspar are back in their homes, I presume, and Akota is being celebrated by the Seraph people and the former Inhabitants of The Kingdom of Gold. And by the way, passing the ring to him has made all the difference for his people. You have shared the donum, and you have yet to realize your brilliance in doing so."

Elias smiled, but he quickly looked down at the splintering planks below. Zoltan felt his angst and wanted to comfort him.

"Oh yes, you may long for them and feel you are missing out—but you are not truly missing out as you are where you are supposed to be—that's the difference. Elias, do not pine for what was or what you think is, nor reach for what you think might be. It is today that matters as we may, most assuredly, count the days we have lived, but we cannot even attempt to count the days ahead of us. Life does, indeed, have a starting point for all, but the endpoint is a mystery. But I dare say, life has a habit of going on whether we like it or not—even if we are in it or not," said Zoltan.

Elias said nothing but looked fondly at Zoltan, then turned and stared at the horizon. As he nodded, a wide smile came across his face as Zoltan sipped from the mug. At that moment, a sparkling aqua and sapphire-colored dragonfly landed on Elias' knuckle. Without moving his head, he gazed down at the quiet and majestic creature.

"We must be near land," Elias' eyes lit up as he kept still and looked intently at the dragonfly.

"Elias, I believe you are correct. That little fellow reminds me of a story I was once told. A story that others have passed down over many years and, as time so masterfully can do, has gobbled up the author's name. Would you like to hear a story?"

Elias faced Zoltan and looked into his eyes. He couldn't help Zoltan's allure as he looked into the recesses of his pupils. The eyes that have seen a thousand years. The eyes that have looked deep inside of him. Elias nodded and smiled.

"A time not so long ago, there was a pond like any other pond—perhaps like the ones around your home or mine. Do you know the kind of pond I speak of?"

"Sure, Zoltan, go on."

"Okay then... in the muddy water under the lily pads, there lived a little neighborhood of water bugs—cute little things. This tiny community lived a simple and predictable life in the murky water. Little concerned them, for the most part, so they were happy creatures. As it is with any community, sadness would come at peculiar times. On occasion, and without warning, a water bug would journey up the stem of a lily pad. To an onlooker in the water bug community, this was not a good sign."

"So the water bug crawled up the stem of a water lily—how is that sad?" asked Elias.

"Well, Elias, all the water bugs knew was that when they saw one of their own make the climb, their friend or family member would never be seen again." Zoltan paused and looked away.

"That's not much of a story. So the water bug climbed up the stem, and a hungry bird ate it. Great story, Zoltan," Elias said, shaking his head.

"Elias, my boy, that is not the end of the story—far from it. Would you allow me to proceed?"

Elias nodded. "Sorry."

"Okay then. The water bugs knew they would never see their friend again. They, like you, thought the worst. They thought their friend was dead.

As it so happened one day, and with no warning to his family or friends, the littlest of water bugs felt an overpowering yearning to journey up that stem. However, he was determined to return to the community and tell his family and friends what he found on the other side. They pleaded with him not to go, but he did anyway. He began to climb the stem. When he reached the surface of the water, he journeyed out of the water onto a lily pad. Because of his climb, he was very tired, and the sun felt good. So the little water bug decided he must close his weary eyes and sleep.

During his nap, he changed. When he woke, he had turned into a beautiful aqua and sapphire dragonfly with graceful wings and a slender body created for flying. Therefore, that's exactly what he did. He soared high above and looked at all below him. He skirted downward and skimmed the surface of the water. He saw new worlds in all its beauty. His perspective was new and fresh—one he thought never existed before that fateful day.

One day, while resting on the arm of a boy, he thought of his friends and family and how they must think he was now dead. It reminded him that he desperately wanted to tell them otherwise and share with them the joy he had found. He hovered over the surface of the water where his family and friends lived, and he could barely make out the little community below. The water was murky that day. He attempted to fly through the surface of the water, but when he tried to reemerge into the water, he could not. He tried and tried and tried to break the surface of the water to no avail. He could see the water bugs below as they continued their simple life. He wanted to explain how he was alive and how wonderful life really was. He wanted to talk about the fulfillment he felt.

Attempt after attempt, he thought differently about telling them and began to understand he was now in the place where he should be. He hoped that their time would come and they, too, would realize that they have wings and one day they would join him. With one last look, he knew what he had to do, and he took to flight, never to allow the past to hold him back. He knew he had to taste the wonders of what today brings."

"So, I'm the dragonfly?" Elias smugly asked.

"You? Maybe the both of us—our friends, too, perchance. But the story, albeit simple, tells more. Think about it."

"I see where it is about living and becoming, but it is also about death. Right?"

"Oh, Elias, it is for you to grapple with—let us speak of it no more."

A huge smooth swell, the size of a modest house, mildly rolled under the lifeboat, placing them high above. As soon as they were at the pinnacle, they descended to a level where all they could see around them was a wall of water. As they evened out, the clouds vanished, and the placid wave slowly moved further away. Many smaller ones rapidly made their presence known as they slapped the boat in all directions. Elias and Zoltan held tight to the sides of the craft until all was calm.

"What was that all about?" Elias said.

"My boy, look over your shoulder, and you will see."

Elias turned, and a good five or six sea miles before them was an iridescent glow the size of a small island of purples, blues, and red. It twinkled in the bright sunlight. Like the waves, the oddity seemed to be covering something as its hues swayed and fluttered to greens, yellows, and orange. It was a magnificent sight.

"Wow! I've never seen anything like it before," said Elias.

"Nor I...nor I."

"What do you think it is, Zoltan?"

"There's nothing like a good mystery than one that is about to unfold in front of our very eyes. Let's wait and see."

As they got closer to the spectacle, they noticed that around the edges of the colors and lights seemed to unravel. Specs, as they thought, were drifting away, and as they did, the two saw rocks, trees, and a mountain.

"Zoltan, they're dragonflies. Millions of dragonflies."

"So they are. Very interesting," Zoltan said, leaning toward Elias. "There is something I must tell you."

6
Fear

Zoltan's faint smile had vanished, and his forehead wrinkled as he continued, "Elias, look at me—it is now time I should tell you that morsel of information that I mentioned a short time ago."

"Yes, Zoltan," Elias sat up and looked toward the old man with curiosity.

"There's a new evil vibration in the Under World that surpasses the malevolence of Ordak."

"What do you mean? Something worse than Ordak. But how?"

"I was able to detect Hibush's plans that day when I read the billowing smoke from the goldsmith's factory. If that Pixie has not done so already, he plans to extract the evil and dark forces from our nemesis, and with his own brand of wickedness, he is headed to that very island." Zoltan said, pointing to the horizon.

"How could it be? I mean, it doesn't make sense."

"I ask, how could it *not* be? I've known nature for millennia; I have seen terrible and hideous things, and these terrible and hideous things run their course, and other malefic powers ooze up to replace them. I have a hunch the Pixie is doing all he can to extract Ordak's powers. This is why the cycle seems to never end. That doesn't mean we give into this dark power, and we must always be vigilant as this force morphs and changes and always keep the good, guessing." Zoltan said.

"But by the likes of Hibush—the Pixie?" Elias asked. "I mean, he's a Pixie."

"Oh yes, my boy. I have seen far worse in history. Far weaker and less significant beings come to power. In fact, the cruelest to rule is by far the lowest—the narcissistic. This is a flaw in the larger scheme of things where a soul is corrupted, and it taps into the worst and darkest corners of man's core to bind souls with empty or foul promises. Their fuel is fear."

"Aren't we smarter than that? I mean, man falls in this...this trap, and as soon as you think it is getting better, it...gosh, it seems like a lesson easy enough to learn," Elias said, shaking his head and looking at the island looming larger with each wave.

"One would think...evil and fear come in many forms. That is one thing man doesn't quite understand about himself. It isn't what a being appears to be; it is what they possess, whether that be love or fear—fear covers the gamut of all the cosmic negative energy."

"Fear? What do you mean? I'm fearful of a Black Widow spider and, well, lightning."

"Lightening? Hmmm. I would have never known that as you handled it quite spectacularly as you brought down Ordak."

"I didn't think about it and did what I had to do."

"Exactly! But I'm talking about another kind of fear. The fear I am talking about, Elias, is a bit different. I'll explain it this way. Love is love. It is nothing more than what it is. It is pure and contains nothing but—love.

It is the most powerful energy in the cosmos. Fear, on the other hand, is love's polar opposite."

"It is? What about hate?"

"Very good question, but as I see it, we *fear* something, and then we *hate* it. First, we fear something, and then we become closed-minded. We fear something, and we become cynical, or we avoid whatever it is we fear. The better choice is to look fear in the eyes and conquer it and not give in to it, just like you did when confronted with lightning. It is when we fear something so much that we give up any chance for love."

"If it never ends, why do anything about it? It's time for me to go home. Zoltan, this is never going to end." Elias looked off away from the island. He saw nothing but the vastness of the sea and imagined a completely different course.

Zoltan put his hand on Elias' shoulder. "I cannot see in the future, but this I know. We must always be vigilant and do what is best; if we do, the future is set. Although we all have choices for the good, we have only one choice to make." said Zoltan.

"Zoltan, I don't understand. Why would he come here...to this island? What's so special about this island?" Elias asked as he combed his fingers through his long hair.

"This island is beyond powerful. It has extraordinary forces that deliver delight one moment and immense anguish the next. It is a place of hidden or secret powers that only the astute may detect. It is perhaps the secret forces of the cosmos that live on that island that Hibush is in search of one in particular—a power he has determined will make him unstoppable."

"Unstoppable?"

"I'm afraid so, Elias. Very few know of this place, but those who do and dare to walk upon it either gain from it or succumb to it as it has devoured many before. If you cannot see the signs or harness the powers it possesses, your future is bleak," Zoltan said with a somberness that Elias had never seen in his friend.

"So that's what happened to Killybegs and his crew," Elias mumbled in awe.

"Killybegs!" Zoltan sat up and leaned toward Elias.

"Do you know who I'm talking about?"

"I would say so...he and his ship, the Amaranthine, was the last voyage to the Isle of Eahta."

"Gosh, that was a long time ago—1667, according to the journal entry I read. It's right over there."

"Where? Let me see."

Elias opened the box, pulled out the yellowed parchment, and handed it to Zoltan. The moment he laid eyes on it, Zoltan said, "Yes, Killybegs and his men perished the very last time the Isle of Eahta surfaced."

"Huh? What do you mean?" Elias blurted as he slowly turned and sat in front of Zoltan.

"Yes—the island surfaces at will, so it seems, and once it does, it stays above the sea for only seven days before it is yanked back under on the eighth. Killybegs was here no more than two weeks ago—maybe three," Zoltan said as one eyebrow went up, and he gave Elias a slight nod.

"What? How do you know for sure?"

"Elias, trust me on this."

"But Zoltan, it's not 1667."

"I told you that time means nothing on these waters near Eahta," Zoltan said.

"How...how? How could that happen?"

"This island holds a power that can carry out monstrous misdeeds. Its true nature is lost on humanity, I dare say."

"So this island and the power it has is evil?" Elias asked, looking toward the island as they were getting closer.

"Surprisingly, the answer to that is no," Zoltan said.

Elias shook his head. "I don't get it. I mean..."

"Consider it a benevolent power that, in the wrong hands, may become sickened."

"Huh?"

"Elias, you must enter the Temple, but getting there is the trick. Getting there is the key, as the experience is everything. Once there, you must unlock the chamber by the seventh day and protect the Elixir of Life from one who plans to use it for their own evil purposes," Zoltan said.

"If that's it, it seems easy enough, but I need a key, don't I? You said I have to unlock the chamber," Elias asked.

"Oh yes, I was waiting for that question. I assume you will find a key along the way...and as far as the seventh day—when the eighth day rings in, the island will sink back into the water from which it emerged, preserving most beings on its surface. Most times, the people live through the ordeal and never leave the island from that day on while others perish due to their sheer panic."

Beginning to fidget, Elias said, "Okay, so you need to fill in some major blanks for me. I mean, I'm supposed to unlock the chamber where the Elixir of Life is before the island, and everyone on it sinks? When I'm done, how do I escape?

"That, my boy, is all I know. But do not become despondent as you will learn to navigate your way around the island while here, and you will learn how to escape its inevitable and scheduled submersion. You do have a boat," Zoltan gently pounded on one side of the craft and followed with a smile. "Oh, and I have this," He reached for his breast pocket. "I have something... now where did it go? Oh my...Nattymama gave me a page out of a book that you must present to Shin."

"Who? Is that a person?"

"Shin. He lives on the island and is a sorcerer of sorcerers, but he will only help you if he has proof of who you say you are. He will not divulge the secrets of the cosmos to just anyone as he is one of the protectors of the Elixir...but it appears I have lost it."

"Zoltan, I'm not sure you are aware of this, but everything you've told me is bad news. I mean, I have seven days to find a temple and unlock the chamber to protect the Elixir. It could take me days to find it, and at the same time, I need to prevent Hibush from getting there first—all without a map, a key, or this page of the book that Nattymama gave you. I'm just not feeling very good about this."

"I believe you have a wonderful grasp of what you need to do. I think it is best to jump in and start—oh, I can't state it enough, but by finding Shin, he will help you solve many of the mysteries you ask about," Zoltan said with a faint smile and a wink.

"Do you have any other surprises for me?"

Zoltan paused, placed his hand over his chin, and looked up. "No, that about does it."

Elias took a moment and stared at the island and then at Zoltan. He knew that Zoltan did not always have all the answers at one time, but he knew he was always there to help him. His journeys thus far have been fraught with challenges that he had learned to overcome, so Elias had the confidence, at least he hoped he did, to take on this mighty task. He viewed it as a 'task' as he knew that if he thought that all of humanity depended on him, he would not be able to leave the boat.

"Zoltan, I'm ready. I can do this."

"That, my good boy, is music to my ears. The answers you ask will come in time—believe me. You are *the one*, but you are not alone." said Zoltan.

Elias turned to watch the island become clearer as the dragonflies scattered and the full sun shone down on all in front of him. Catching his attention above, he saw the great Turul for the first time since leaving the Kingdom of Gold. He was gliding and seemed to be in control of the skies.

"Zoltan, seeing the Turul is a good sign," Elias said, turning to look at Zoltan, but when he did, Zoltan had vanished.

7

Day One on the Isle of Eahta

Almost rubbing the bottom of the surf, Elias jumped out of the boat, and the water was up to his knees. The water gushed into his boots. Elias pulled the boat as close to shore as he could. He used the long rope to tie it around a large boulder. Scratching his head, he first looked to his right and then his left. He puffed up his cheeks and let out all the air that filled his lungs. "I'm here," he hollered to no one.

A bit overwhelmed and distracted by his new surroundings, he plopped on the sand and yanked off his wet boots. Digging his hands into the warm, white sand, it felt soft like silk. He then dug his toes into the powdery beach as he had never experienced the feeling of sand on his skin. The sand was smooth and soothing, unlike the rocky and clay-rich soil he was used to back home. Thinking about it, he had never been on a boat in a sea or an ocean and had never been on a sandy beach. He sat in awe, looking at the endless waves seemingly coming from nowhere and crashing right before him. The white foam came up to his toes and sped out, only to come up even further next time as he sprung up on all fours and scurried backward like a crab before the wave returned. His thoughts wandered as the mesmerizing waves gushed in and out. He knew he was looking back into history and into the future at the same time—as this same scene before him had played out for millions of years before that very moment and will continue for the next million. The roar, the pounding of the sea, and the sight were constant, and the memory of that moment would last his lifetime.

Resting for a few minutes, he used his heels to dig in the sand until he felt a coolness surrounding his feet. Leaning back on his elbows, he looked up to the blue sky and took a few deep breaths as he knew that his rest could only be for a few minutes. He had to continue his journey in a place that was foreign, just like the one he had just come from in the Under World. *Am I still in the Under World? Is this someplace else?*

He breathed in deeply, pulled his knees up to his chest, and wondered why he was thrust into this adventure, as it was nothing he had asked for. He felt conflicted. On one hand, he was ready for his charge, and on the other hand, he was ready to go home. He knew, though, that he was being called for greater things—the same as everyone, Zoltan would remind him, but not everyone owns up to their greater calling. This reminder didn't make him feel much better. He began to feel nervous as everything was new, and the stakes were now overpowering his thoughts. He took a moment to meditate as he was taught by the great mystic Tas and knew this would empower him going forward.

◆ ◆ ◆

The narrow beach was only about fifteen meters wide before it reached the thick green vegetation and trees. These lush, colorful woods were like none he had seen before. The grass was as tall as trees, and the trees were full of flowers and vines. Because of this new encounter, Elias was curious about all around him. He scanned everything in all directions. For such a small island, all he could see was sand to one side, to the other, a strange forest, leaving only the sea he had just come from. He spotted crabs running erratically and burying themselves in the sand whenever he approached them. In unison, he saw a flock of tiny, long-legged birds with skinny beaks running together at the edge of the water. It made him chuckle. There was a long row of seashells, and one captured his attention.

He scooped it up and took a moment to give it a good look. It was a beautiful fan-shaped shell with all the colors of a sunset. He tucked it into a pocket.

So now what? Gosh, I wonder if Cimbora is here somewhere. I really miss him. He looked around again as if he would spot his dog but shook his head and stood for a moment looking at the vastness of the sea. *Zoltan said I would meet up with Cimbora and Kelsa soon.*

Knowing he had better start his journey, Elias went back to the boat and pulled out the Captain's journal, thinking he'd find a few more clues. He frantically thumbed through the pages, but it was mostly blank parchment, or the water had smeared the ink in some places. The recent pleasures he had just enjoyed had been flushed away as the reality of the situation hung heavy in his heart. Feeling a frustration churning and coming from nowhere, he began tearing out the pages, one by one. With his weariness getting the best of him, he flung the book to the other side of the craft, hitting hard on the splintered wall of the boat. To his surprise, the weather-battened binding broke in half. What slid from the leather casing was a long rolled up piece of parchment.

"What could that be?" he said under his breath, rushed to where it lay, and grabbed it. Unrolling it, he turned it one way and then the other. "A page of a book, it looks like...it's got a map of this place and...and that must be the Temple," he said, pointing to a large square with a circle in it that appeared to be next to a large body of water within the island. "So, in the next seven days, I've got to find where the chamber door is in that building– but first, the key – and I will be able to uncover what it is that Hibush and Killybegs, and so many others have been searching for."

This was all he needed to turn his sudden jolt of anxiety into that of renewed hope. Memorizing the map as best as he could at the moment, he saw four paths that led from the shore to the Temple. *Which path is the best one to take? Is one, I wonder, more dangerous than another, or is one path more direct? I just can't tell looking at this.* He looked at the island and back down at the yellowed page. His forehead wrinkled, and he pursed his lips. Looking back at the island, he folded up the map and stuffed it in his back pocket. He then grabbed his dagger and fastened it to his belt. As he did from time to time, he placed his palm over the amulet that never left his neck. He hopped out of the boat, sloshed up to the shore, and just then, he saw the Turul emerge from a faint and wispy cloud. She headed east. "So that's the way I'm headed too," he said and swooped up his boots, tied the laces together, and flung them over one shoulder. "All I know is that I've got to get to the chamber door before Hibush."

Barefoot, he continued down the shoreline but saw nothing that even remotely looked like an opening for one of the four paths into the thick, dense brush. The forest looked fresh and untouched as it was clearly undisturbed. It looked like no one or anything had entered the thick vegetation wherever he looked. He peered up to the sky to find the Turul, but this time, she was nowhere to be found. The map clearly showed four entrances—four paths, so he kept walking at a good pace with his eye on the tall, odd-looking, and colorful trees. He saw bamboo-like stalks mixed with thick plants that looked like giant blades of colorful grass—every color imaginable. From his vantage point, he still could not see very far ahead.

In the distance, a figure came into view, but it was too small to make sense of it. "Is that a person?" He placed his hand above his eyes like a visor to block the glaring sun. He picked up his pace to a jog. "Yeah, that's a person alright." As he got closer, he was able to determine that she was tall with long, flowing hair. She sat very still in the sand. Her hands were clasping her knees, and she gazed at the choppy sea, almost in a trance, as the increasing gray layers of clouds were being tugged by an invisible force. Elias picked up his pace even more and ran up to approach her.

As not to startle her, he called out when he was about fifty paces away. "Ah, ah, ma'am, my boat just washed me up to the shore about a kilometer west of here and...".

Her stare was fixed outward, and the breeze captured her dark curls and sent them into her face as she interrupted Elias and said, "I can't recall when the last boat crashed here—on this side of the island. Just on the rocky side. No one escapes the rocky side."

Confused by her response, Elias said, "I see. But I was wondering if you could help me find my way around this island."

"I gave up on being found quite some time ago. I've lost all track of time, and in fact, time means nothing, nothing at all—at least here."

She turned from her attention to the sea to size up Elias. Sparkling in the sun, she saw the amulet around his neck. "I now know who you are. Word gets around, even here on Eahta."

"I am Elias—I'm nobody special. I mean, I'm not famous or anything. I'm not sure why you would know me." Pulling the amulet away from his chest, he looked at it. "I guess the amulet must be known to many."

"Humility will always, ALWAYS, eclipse arrogance. You, I can tell, are growing with dignity and do not need evidence of admiration from hordes of people. The endless vibration you have sent into the cosmos is full of light and hope, which is all mere mortals need. If they only believed that."

"That's really nice of you, but I'm not sure about all that. I'm an artist—I paint—and to tell you the truth, I really want others to like and want my paintings. So. I am not so humble after all."

"Your art is part of you, and you are part of it. I suspect that you want others to appreciate the same wonders you have experienced, and as these wonders are part of you, the appreciation is quite welcome, am I right?"

"Hmmm, yeah—pretty much. I never thought of it that way."

"You would continue to paint no matter what, am I right?"

"Yeah, I guess I would." Elias' smile stretched across his face.

"But as we speak, we are getting closer to the eighth day," she said.

"Oh yeah. So, can you help me figure out how to get around this place?"

"Certainly. There's a village, if you can call it that, through the forest right behind us. I would watch my step with those that live there."

Elias turned and saw a large opening in the lush foliage. "Oh, so *there's* an entrance. I was beginning to wonder."

"Yes, dear boy, there is always an entrance—remember that. That passageway takes you deeper into this wonderous but forsaken place. Once you are here, you never—NEVER—leave. I've seen them come but have never seen them go. Ships and boats of all kinds have come this way—most crashed on the rocky shore on the opposite side of the island—near the Temple. In fact, you are the first one to come ashore on this side of this island. As I've said, I've been here a long time, too, so I know." She slowly turned her head to look at the sea.

"Ah, yes, ma'am. I bet you do."

She looked down the shoreline where he had come from and asked, "So you're saying you have a boat—a boat that can sail, and it is right up the shore?" She pointed.

With the stranger's question, Elias felt like he suddenly had a rock in his stomach. "I don't want to lie to you, but yes, it is intact, um, it's seaworthy. If you help me, I can take you back with me if that's what you want."

She smiled, and as she did, her face appeared bright, "That's very kind of you, but that's not why I ask. Your invitation is most generous, and I will never forget your offer. I'm happy to help you if I can, but I don't need to go anywhere. As I said only a moment ago, no one on this island can leave it."

"No one?"

"If you leave by the eighth day on your boat, yes, you are safe."

"I don't get it. Did they know that? Were all their ships wrecked beyond repair?"

"Although those on this island all came from different boats and at different times, they have all struggled to find a way to get home. I was on my way to be with my new husband when life changed. Our lives can shift like the sand before us. Here, time has forgotten us. Once the eighth day came, we were here for good—those of us who made it."

"Ma'am, I'm sorry, but you didn't answer my question. What do you mean?" asked Elias.

"I hope things will be different for you—please don't get me wrong."

"I need to know more. What do you mean about *never leaving* this place? And... and some don't make it. I plan to make it out of here."

She went from a listless bearing to straightening her back and said, "Okay, since I think you are going to ask me a hundred questions, let's talk about whatever it is that you want to talk about." She interrupted herself and started over in a more pleasant manner. "My name is Ambrosia, let's chat, my dear."

"You know my name already, but it is nice to know yours—nice to meet you," Elias said, holding out his hand. She looked at it and back into his eyes.

"Nice to meet you, too. Now I am putting the pieces together... please sit—pull up some sand, and let's talk."

Elias felt his body tense up but thought his best hope at that moment was to talk with her to see how she might be able to help him. He sat at her side. The breeze kicked up, but it felt good as he was hot from plowing through the sand in the broiling rays of the sun.

"You said that time has forgotten you and that no one wants to or can leave. What's so special about this place? I mean, it is pretty, from the beach to the colorful forest to the beautiful sky, but why?"

"You are correct. It *is* special, but nothing, *nothing*, is special forever. Seven days, perhaps. Those who came here didn't know that they must leave before the eighth day rang in, but little did that matter as our ships and boats were damaged. Most were mangled beyond repair."

"So no one could repair them in time?" he said, knowing the answer.

"Thinking that we had all the time in the world to make our crafts seaworthy again, we just didn't know that was the way of Eahta. Strangely, we did feel a sense of happiness, and those who were sick for one reason or another were now well. We felt the powers of this place and thought in time, we'd be rescued."

"I've heard of the powers here, but it seems a bit fuzzy to me."

"Oh, yes. I have become part of the Isle of Eahta, like the white smooth sand. Its power is like no other. On the eighth day, the island slips back into the sea, and it randomly emerges from time to time. Once that happens, anyone here is imprisoned to the beauty of this place and is here to stay."

"What!"

"Yes, I'm afraid so. I have told every new bright-eyed visitor, but they either do not believe me or cannot find a way out as they have waited far too long."

"What becomes of the people of the island? You say it 'slips back into the sea.'"

"Perhaps we go into a protected sleep, or perhaps something else protects us, but whatever happens, we are not hurt. I should say that those of us who do not panic and fight the island are never hurt. It is when those who have no way off and try to swim away—are pulled under the sea and are never seen again.

"Wow. Makes sense, though."

"Most of those who become 'part of the island' become *different* in some way. This is part of the power of this island."

"What do you mean—become *different*?"

62

"We don't have time to delve into that. You must get somewhere apparently and get back to your boat in time to safely leave Eahta, am I correct?"

"Yes, I'm under the clock."

"And Elias, remember what I said about time, as time means *nothing* here. So let me remind you that you are safe if you turn around, find your boat, and set sail before the eighth day," she said, turning and looking directly into Elias' eyes, "and if you're smart and you look smart enough, I would do exactly what I just told you. Waste no more time and leave this place."

"I'm here to do something and can't leave until I've done it. It is something that I *must* do. But I'm sure I can do it in seven days."

Ambrosia laughed, and when she stopped, she began to laugh louder. Elias was puzzled at what he said that was so funny. "What did I say? Why are you laughing?"

"Oh Elias—I just told you that time means nothing on Eahta."

"You also said that I have seven days before the island sinks in the ocean."

"Yes, but if I remember correctly, your day is twenty-four hours long, and the sun comes up—the sun goes down, and the people back home start all over again."

"Yeah, that's a day where I come from...so what's a day here?"

"Maybe half that. Yes, it's half that, give or take. The problem is the sun doesn't set, but a lovely moon appears in the sky from time to time. It, however, has nothing to do with how long a day lasts. It never gets dark, and we do not sleep as there is no need. Eating is optional as we don't get hungry."

"This is just too strange. I'm going to get done what I need to do and get out of here." Elias pushed out his bottom lip and blew out his breath as his bangs fluttered in all directions. "So this is why people don't leave or can't leave or get lost here. It's like a trap."

"Now you know." Ambrosia stood and brushed the sand from the back of her legs. She faced the sea.

"Now I know," Elias said in a deflated tone. "So, if I think about it, I am in the middle of my first day." He jumped up and stood next to her, looking to the horizon.

"I wish I could help you with the math, but I don't know how long you've been here. Let me ask you about something you said."

"Sure, but I don't have much time, or whatever I should call it—*time that is.*"

"What is it that you must do before you may leave? You, too, are speaking to me in riddles."

"I don't mean to, but...okay, here it goes—see, there's a Pixie that has learned and absorbed all the powers of Ordak, and he wants to take over the cosmos; he thinks all he needs is the Elixir of Life to do it."

"I see, I see. So you are a warrior of sorts?" she asked with indifference. "You are here to save the cosmos from a Pixie?" she asked as she tried to hold back her laughter.

"When you say it that way, it doesn't sound that serious, but believe me, it is. I am here to protect the Elixir of Life. If I do that, the Pixie is nothing."

Ambrosia took a few steps closer to the sea and, again, sat. "And you want a sip, I bet, while you are saving the cosmos?"

"No!" He squatted in front of her and looked directly at her. "As I said, I want to get this done and go home. I am not a warrior; I do not want a sip, but I have had to confront Ordak before, and this could be worse—I know." He spun on one foot, plopped onto the sand, and closed his eyes.

"Well, you've convinced me you are telling the truth, and I'm quite good at reading those who show up on this island. I have been *reading* folks for a long time."

"Thanks—I am telling you the truth, and with only seven days, or whatever I have, to get to the Temple before *he* gets there and the island sinks, I've got to work fast."

"Elias, you will find many obstacles from here to there, and if you make it, you will be one of the few over the millennia to have done so. It takes more than navigating the terrain. It has to do with who you are. Do you want to take that wickedly slim chance of getting there in one piece?"

"The Pixie's got to be stopped, and I'm here now – so there's no turning back. Yeah, I've got to do this." A large wave pounded the beach and rode all the way up to where they were sitting.

"I thought so but wanted to ask you one last time. Something tells me you can do it...something tells me that there is no stopping you." Ambrosia smiled as she brushed her hands together, and the sand took flight in the calm breeze.

"Can you tell me anything else?"

"Young Elias, although I like you and you are living your legend, I can only tell you so much."

"I'm living my what? *Legend*? C'mon."

"Yes, my dear boy. If you think about it, life for you is very different."

"Well, yes."

"Your deeds have been remembered, and you are known... but still a stranger to me. I am one of the few who protects this island, so I can only help you so much. I have seen many who have evil in their hearts attempt to find the Elixir, so I must be careful."

"I understand. I should go now."

Ambrosia quickly changed her mind. "Wait, Elias. Perhaps I can share more as I believe you, and if you are truly the chosen one, you will succeed. I believe you are."

Elias' eyes lit up. "So what else can you tell me?"

"Be prepared to challenge the protectors of the Temple, and they aren't just monsters. Sometimes, the 'protectors' are not living beings but are deterrents for you to overcome. So use your ingenuity—your brain—and your heart to find a way to the chamber door."

"I know I need to find a key to unlock the door, right?"

"Yes, but keys are not just what you find on a ring. Think of other ways. Think of this island's name."

"Huh? Eahta? I have no idea what the name means."

"It means eight."

"Oh! Makes sense."

"Think of seven days, Elias."

"Oh, I got it so..."

"Oops, I have said too much," she said with a grin and a wink. "There are two other numbers. But I do not know them. The one making the journey must search for those, and it is not for those who merely talk about the journey. Find Shin. He's in the village."

"Of course. Zoltan told me the same thing. So...what else can you tell me?"

"No more."

"Yeah, I thought I might be pressing my luck right now."

"I am sorry, but I walk a fine line, and I must protect Eahta from the rest of humanity. You must understand that if mere mortals and other creatures knew the secrets here, like the Pixie, it would be catastrophic—trust me on that."

"I'm ready, but this isn't going to be easy, I can tell."

"Please remember, there are always zigzags to everything in our lives. It is never a straight line. Nothing is a sure bet. There is no good luck or bad. We must learn to find the good and learn to address the bad."

"Okay, thanks. I know you are trying to help me, but during our conversation, it seems to become clear, but there's so much to remember it gets lost or jumbled."

She smiled and said, "Exactly. Not all is clear all the time; the light will be bright when you need it most. Things, many times, have a way of sorting themselves out."

"Thanks, but I'll need my boat, so I hope it's there when I return."

"As I said, none of the existing inhabitants care about your boat. But if a new arrival is in search of a way off, your boat is vulnerable."

"Hmmm, it's too big for me to pull it ashore and hide it, so I can only hope for the best."

"I think you are right about that. That's all anyone can do. Since all others have come from the other, rocky side of the island, they may never know your boat exists—and if I meet up with a Pixie, most assuredly, I will never tell," said Ambrosia.

"Thanks. That's nice of you, but why?"

"I like you, Elias—because I like you. Need I say more?"

Elias looked away and blushed. He cleared his throat and turned to her, trying to look stern, "Of the four paths leading me closer to the Temple, what's the best one to take?" Elias began to pull on his boots and strap his dagger to his left boot.

"Why, of course, the path that's before you in the here and now. No need to question it or look any further."

With that advice, Elias bid her adieu and began walking to the entrance of the forest where the path began. He turned to wave to

Ambrosia, but she was walking out into the water. The breeze whipped through her flowing gown as she got past the foam of the water. Elias stopped and watched her dive in. Puzzled, he poked his head forward with a slight tilt as he waited for her to surface. His attention shifted. Way out in the sea, he saw a sea serpent emerge and then dip below the surface. "I hope she'll be okay."

8
Cimbora

Heading down the path, Elias was leaving the sandy beach and the tang of the salty sea that hung on the breeze. Within the first few moments, the sound of the pounding waves of the sea was all but silenced as it was swallowed by the forest. Like a door suddenly closing, each step of the path engulfed him in a bright palette of colors that was slowly turning into a dark and hushed tunnel of thick vegetation. He could see only a ribbon of blue sky and dappled beams of light finding their way through the dense canopy. It was cool, and the mixture of various exotic plants added a rich sweetness to the air, replacing that of the sea. The path was straight without the slightest of bends as far as he could tell. Mud-packed and smooth, the route was narrow and was only for traveling by foot as it was only the width of Elias' arm span. It was oddly still and without even the slightest of breezes due to the giant blades of grass and bamboo. *This is nothing like what I am used to,* he thought. The muscles of his shoulders were tense, and he was biting his bottom lip as he trudged on. His ears and eyes were focused as he was ready for anything that might cross his path. Other than his footsteps, all was quiet.

"I wonder where this village is that Ambrosia talked about. Everyone seems to know Shin. She seemed to be telling the truth—I hope," Elias said out loud. He plodded further, but now, in the distance ahead of him, he heard something stirring in the deep brush. He paused firmly in his tracks as if that would help amplify the sound. Looking in all directions, he zeroed in on where he thought the rustling was coming from. He crouched down and reached for his dagger that was fastened to his boot. Eyes darting from side to side, he wiggled his fingers above the dagger's handle as he waited. Beads of sweat formed on his forehead, and he felt a lump in his throat. Only a few seconds later, the rustling faded as if it was soaked up by the enormous leafy brush. He slowly stood straight, rubbed his hand across his forehead, and resumed his travels. Now, however, he kept his eyes and ears even more acutely attuned to all around him.

I wish I knew where Kelsa and Cimbora were. Zoltan said that he sent them where I will see them soon, but he's not always precise with his sorcery—I don't think he meant to land me in that boat, and I'm pretty sure he DID mean to land IN THE BOAT when he showed up out of the blue—AND not in the sea.

Elias walked another quarter of an hour or so and decided to plop down right in the middle of the path to rest. The ground was cool as he sprawled out, leaning back on his elbows. He began to talk out loud, looking side to side. "I could use a swig of water. I hope I find that village soon, or someone's gonna find me dried up on this stupid path. It won't be pretty."

Before Elias could think of his next thought, he heard a loud crunch and swoosh coming from the green wall that surrounded him. Stunned, he couldn't get to his feet before a black blur of a creature jumped on him—and began to lick his face. "Cimbora! It's you. Buddy—oh my gosh! You're here." Cimbora's tongue was moving faster than the speed of sound, and the two rolled around as Elias laughed so hard that he thought his sides were going to burst wide open. Cimbora joined in with a few short, welcoming barks followed by panting.

Worn out, Elias laid squarely on his back with legs and arms spread eagle, and Cimbora joined him at his side, still panting with his tongue out to one side. Elias looked to his friend and gently nodded with a smile that took up much of his face. Pulling himself up to one elbow and combing his fingers through his hair, Elias realized that there was something around Cimbora's neck. It was a soft leather canteen full of fresh water. "Ah, boy, I can always count on you." Elias pulled off the canteen and downed a few swigs.

"So buddy, did you come here with Kelsa?"

Cimbora barked three or four times. With that, Elias knew that Kelsa was on the island—but where? "Do you know where she is?" Cimbora tilted his head from side to side as if he was thinking about his answer. He sniffed in one direction and then another. "Would you be able to find her?" Cimbora answered with a short bark. "Good! Let's go". With that, Elias jumped to his feet as they headed further down the path.

They must have journeyed another kilometer when they saw a clearing that shed a blue, green glow. The glow brightened and lost its color as they got closer. "So that's where the people live on this island. Let's go, Cimbora." They picked up the pace and found themselves at the end of a road off the path that led to only one place, and that was the village. Elias saw a peculiar cluster of buildings that were arranged like a main street of a town. No more than a city block long, the road was wide, and its surface was made up of a variety of stones—but in the same way, it started on one end; that's how it ended—it led nowhere.

The buildings were all different, but they were all attached. They were out of place to be stuck in the middle of an island. Some looked like they could have been in a city, and others looked like rural cottages. Who lived here? In the very middle of the road was a circle that was the center of town. One building stood out as it seemed to be the only place where he saw strange beings going in and out. It was some kind of meeting house. The only sounds he heard came from this place, but nothing he heard sounded like words. Elias looked down at Cimbora. "Is that where she is?" Cimbora made a few short whinnying sounds and shook his head.

"Hmmm. Let's just see what's here, and maybe you can pick up her scent." They began to wander toward the center of the street when, out of nowhere, a thin man wearing a long, colorful kimono ran between them.

He was holding a black box with an image of a lotus blossom emblazoned on the top. Once he shot past them, he peered back, but with lightning speed, he turned and ran into one of the houses. As the door slammed, Cimbora let out a long howl.

"Is Kelsa in there, boy?

Cimbora ran to the house, and with his wet nose only inches from the door, he began to bark. Right behind him, Elias joined him and banged on the door. Almost instantly, the man slowly opened the door and poked out his head.

"Elias?"

"Yes, and this is Cimbora. Wait! How do you know who I am?"

"Well, young man," he said, looking into Elias' eyes, "I have heard everything about you from friends of yours."

"Oh, so it wasn't from some cosmic vibration?" he asked with some sarcasm.

"Huh? Oh, I see. You are being funny...yes, funny."

"Sorry. But you said, friends?"

"Why yes. You have a few of those, I believe."

"Would one of them be Kelsa? Is she in here?" Elias stretched out his neck and tried to look inside the house.

"Why yes, yes, she is. Will you come in?"

9
Shin

BAM! The wind came up behind Elias and Cimbora and slammed the wooden door shut behind them. "I must say, you *do* know how to make an entrance, young Elias."

"Sorry about that. So where's Kelsa?" He walked in and looked one way and then another. Full of creepy shadows, the room was poorly lit. There was only one window, but the curtain was pulled, and only one small lamp provided most of the light.

"First things first. Has anyone ever told you that you are quite the impatient one?" Shin shook his head.

"I've heard that before. To tell you the truth, if she's her, I'm not getting why I can't see her now. Where is she?"

"Before we begin, hand it over." Shin walked up to Elias and stood in front of him.

Elias bristled at the harsh order from the man who was supposed to be helpful. "Hand *what* over?"

"It is my understanding that you will present page seventy-two of the ancient book known as <u>The Book of the Land that Doesn't Exist</u>. There are only eight such books that can be accounted for the last time I received word about such things.

"Wait—*what?* I've been there. I had no idea." Elias straightened up and took a step backward.

"That is impossible." Shin turned away and folded his arms against his chest.

"Nattymama sent me there, and that's where I spent time with Tas. I don't have the page you're looking for."

"Tas? Did you say Tas? You mean the mystic, the prophet, the, the ..."

As Shin rambled on, Elias, without being noticed, sauntered around the room and looked for anything that could be a door as his suspicions were growing. This meeting with Shin did not seem right. Paying more attention to his surroundings than to Shin, he pulled back the curtain and looked out. "Tas is a man like any other who stands before us, and we, as he said to me, should just listen. Listen, that's all. I mean, that's what I learned when I asked him to describe himself. He is seriously not into labels."

"Interesting, Elias—*very interesting*. Since you do not have the page, I will ask you questions, and you must answer them precisely. I cannot risk this information to a shape-shifting Sarkany, Pixie, or whatever creature comes knocking. Do you understand?"

"I understand, but I want to know if Kelsa is okay. Why are you keeping her hidden from me?"

Leaning toward Elias and craning his neck, he continued as if he hadn't heard him. "Did he show you the world that we *could* live in?"

"I spent several days there, and he taught me things."

"Things? Tell, tell—what things?"

From a lying position at Elias' feet, Cimbora jumped to all fours. He began to sniff around the room.

"Please call your dog back over here. He may get into some mischief if he's out of your sight. Lovely dog, though, uh huh."

"Mischief? In this small room. Where's the door to the rest of this place, and where is Kelsa?

Shin reached out and grabbed Elias' collar. His face instantly grew hard and cold. He released his hold on Elias, patted his collar, and forced an unsettling smile. "So sorry, my boy, but it has been a troubling day. I assure you Kelsa is fine, but I must be reassured that you are the one you say you are. Please ask your dog to return to you."

"Cimbora, hey boy, come, come." Elias' stomach felt as if he had eaten something sour, and he knew for sure things were not right. He began to think, if this situation went sideways, what should his next move be. He stayed guarded.

Head down, Cimbora inched back to join Elias and Shin, but he looked up to Shin, and Shin reached down to pet him. Cimbora turned and lowered his head.

"Please sit Elias and tell me more of what Tas told you. Tell me about his powers. I heard you acquired some and used them against the great Ordak."

"The great Ordak! What?"

"Oh, I used the wrong word. Ah, ah, we're not speaking in my native tongue. Come and sit at the table near the window where I will open the curtain to let in more light. You may like that, Elias. Yes?"

Elias nodded. They sat.

"The sooner we get this out of the way, the sooner you will be reunited with Kelsa. Please, tell me more."

Elias thought for a moment to decide what he would tell Shin. "Hmmm, Tas said that man and only man live in opposites. Man must have ugly to have beauty, or he has to have evil to know good," he said, looking into Shin's eyes.

"Go on."

"He said man must make sense of these opposites but, more importantly, learn to strike a balance—that kind of thing."

"I see; tell me what else he said. Tell me about his powers—*his magic.*"

Cimbora bounced up to all fours again and began barking at Shin.

"HOLD IT. Suppose *you* are a shape-shifting Pixie. I need proof from you. Enough of this! Where's Kelsa? This is all wrong." Elias pushed away from the table as his chair fell backward to the floor, making a loud thwack.

At that moment, Shin began to grow as his face became contorted. Cimbora's fur stuck up as he reared back and began to bark and growl even louder. Shin's appearance morphed to look like Ordak, and within a few more seconds, the transfiguration was complete. There, standing only inches from Elias, was Ordak. Elias quickly whipped out his dagger and pointed it at him. Ordak remembered that Elias' dagger not only had a sharp blade but also had powers that were unknown to him and ones that he was not ready for in his weakened state.

"Elias, lower your blade, my boy, lower it, and let's talk. As I know the secrets of balancing good and evil, you and I may work together to ensure this balance."

Stunned, Elias stood taller, and his face tightened up as his eyes pierced Ordak, "Don't try to pull that with me! You should be...you should be dead. Where's Hibush? He sucked your powers from you and is on this island somewhere."

With a cackling and shrieking laugh, Ordak said, "Oh, poor Pixie. He made all the wrong moves, as he's such a novice. Kind of like you, Elias. But I have rendered him powerless—oh, he can do whatever a Pixie can do, but he is not capable of the evil I possess."

"Look at you. You are a weak has-been. You may have regained your powers, but your pride was just too much for you as you wasted most of your powers to stomp out Hibush and get to Eahta. You're using your energies to shapeshift, and you don't have it in you to do much else. I'm not afraid of you."

"I am here to remedy that, Elias. The Isle of Eahta is a place of renewal with or without the Elixir—don't you know? That, I would think, is very easy to see and is not a secret I am trying to keep. I intend to find the Elixir before you or anyone else, and once I do, there will be no stopping me. Do you understand me?"

He stepped back, and as he faded, morphing into a gray cloud of smoke, he escaped through the porous wood door. It only took a moment, and he was gone.

Squatting down to Cimbora, Elias said, "Thanks, boy. You knew—you knew. And I bet you caught the scent of Kelsa in this place. There must be a door. Let's figure this thing out."

Elias ran his hands over what appeared to be a flat wall. He felt a seam, and using his fingers, he dug them into the tiny groove. Now certain that he had found a door, he pushed and pushed but couldn't budge, hoping to gain entrance. He barreled his shoulder in the same space, but the door, if it was a door, did not open. It felt like a solid wall. Then, a smile came over his face as he shook his head. He pulled out his dagger, pointed it at the wall, and said, *apereta* and a door materialized and creaked open. "I learned that one from Zoltan."

"Cimbora, I've got to remember that I have a few powers I can use in times like this." Cimbora barked. Elias went to the opening, but it was pitch black. Using his dagger again, he pointed it to the black space and shouted, *illuminare!* With the added light from his dagger, they found stairs going down to a large room. At once, he spotted Kelsa and Shin, he assumed, tied up and gagged. They were sitting on the floor up against the wall. Elias, followed by Cimbora, rushed down the rickety staircase and first pulled Kelsa's gag out and then Shin's.

"Are you okay?" Elias asked them as they both nodded.

"Whew, It's good to see you, Elias—and you too, Cimbora." Cimbora greeted her with a kiss. "Thanks, boy, I knew you and Elias were here somewhere on this island. It was scary, and I had to believe you were on your way. I didn't know what was going to happen to us."

"Keeping it to myself, I thought we were as good as dead as no one would find us here. This is my secret place, and no one knows I have this room," Shin said as he rubbed his wrists.

Elias helped Kelsa to a chair, and Shin followed and fell back into a big, cushioned chair.

"Wait a minute, how do you know Shin? I mean, how did you know to come here?" said Elias.

"We really don't know each other. Zoltan sent me here—to Shin's house. I told him about what you did to the Kingdom of Gold and what the Bee People did to Ordak."

"I know Zoltan, so what Kelsa was telling me made sense," said Shin.

"The more Shin and I talked, the more I learned about this island and the Elixir of Life—unbelievable," Kelsa said.

"Only a moment or two later, we heard this banging on the door," said Shin.

"He answered the door, and some strange man that Shin had never seen before barged in and began pushing us around," said Kelsa.

"Yes, and he used some kind of spell on us, and I was in a thick fog of a daze. That's all I could remember until just a few minutes before you found us," Shin said.

"Oh, you don't know who this stranger is, do you, Kelsa?"

She shook her head and said, "He didn't look familiar to me. After he tied us up, he left us to rot down here. Sitting down here with so much racing in my head, I thought he must have been a shapeshifter—must have been Hibush.

78

"Yes, I told Kelsa that I heard a Pixie named Hibush was on his way to Eahta to steal the Elixir," Shin said.

"Well, he was."

"What? He was? Then who was that?" Kelsa's eyes got wide.

"That was Ordak. I don't know what he looked like to you when he got here, but he is definitely in the flesh or whatever it is that covers his evil body," Elias said, shaking his head.

"WHAT?" Kelsa blurted. "We were taken for fools!"

"Yes, we were. Very good disguise, this Ordak had. He had us fooled or, rather, disarmed us by his unassuming appearance," Shin said as he gave his cheek a few pats of his finger.

"If you can believe Ordak, he said Hibush let his guard down, and then Ordak swooped in to disarm the Pixie. Hibush is not on this island. But Ordak is, but he is weak. I could see the thousand bee stings he got from our friends. He even acknowledged he was on Eahta to regain his strength. He didn't want to fight, but he wanted to get to the Elixir. He fled, but he doesn't know where to find the Elixir. He hoped to get a page out of an ancient book, but Zoltan lost it before he could get it to me. Good thing he lost it."

"What? So you've seen Zoltan?" asked Kelsa.

"Yeah, it's a long story."

Kelsa stood and stretched and then fell back into her chair. "Unless you gave him a clue, Ordak's no closer to the Elixir than the moment he tied us up. I'd say you have some time to work with before he gets there."

Elias turned to Shin. "So you can help us?"

"It is my duty, and it is my honor, Elias," said Shin.

"It's great to hear that. You wouldn't have liked the Shin I first met. I've got to get that image out of my head. Whew! Anyway...but don't you need page seventy-two from <u>The Book of the Land that Doesn't Exist</u> to prove who I am."

"You have already proven who you are, Elias...but I must tell you that I had a visit from the Turul this morning who delivered the page and a note from Nattymama—*that* Zoltan, he's something else. Like you said, as fate had it, he lost the page, and that *was* a good thing. Zoltan is who he is, and I love him," Shin said, followed by friendly laughter, and Elias and Kelsa joined it with a bark or two from Cimbora.

10

Surprise Visitors

Day Two on the Isle of Eahta

With her long wingspan and immense presence in the sky, she circled the Temple and the lush green land that locked it away. The Turul glided with ease, knowing that the sky was hers. She could see from one end of the island to the other, and all pockets of activity were no secret to her. As she flew, she felt the salty air coming off the sea, and her feathers glistened in the sunlight.

Because of her keen vision, she saw a large creature lying unconscious on a boulder and another smaller one sprawled out close by. She swooped down, confirming to herself that she did, in fact, know the creatures in distress. She landed near the large one and tilted her head one way and then another, determining what she should do. With a mojo only she possessed, she merely touched her soft wing feathers to his chest, and by doing so, she awoke Blugwan. Her spell immediately brought him back to health.

As he opened his eyelids with a flutter, the great beast's warm brown eyes glowed as the muscles of the edges of his large mouth lifted his face like the welcoming light that emerges at the dawn of a new day.

"It is so good to see you, Turul. So good."

The Turul bowed her head.

"But what is this place? Is it the Isle of Eahta? You never know when you enter a portal sometimes. They can take you to places you'd rather not go." With a trill and then a tweet, she answered him and then asked a question.

Hearing her question, he looked intently at the Turul, then looked away and spoke. "I thought so. Yes, we were in the Forsaken Sea, and Hibush let me go when we found Ordak; he was nearly dead. I wished we would have left him alone. Anyway, It was a gruesome sight and one I wished I had never seen. I stayed close by but was undetected by the others. I wanted to see what the Pixie was really up to."

With another short trill, a pause, and then a warble, the Turul asked another question.

"Oh, sorry. Nothing doing. Hibush didn't get his powers, but he planned to pull out all the dark forces he could from Ordak, come here, sip the Elixir, and rule supreme over the cosmos. Pitiful, but that was his aim in life—and his downfall." Blugwan sat up straight and pulled his shoulder blades back, and the sounds of his cracking spine were loud. "But little did Hibush know, nor Pewton or me, that Ordak still had enough power bubbling in him. He easily gained back his control over Hibush. Hibush didn't know what hit him," Blugwan said with a chuckle.

With a short trill, the Turul asked more.

"Oh, yeah—sorry. Ordak used a spell and created a portal to take him here—Old Hibush gave him the idea. Knowing that there'd be problems, I jumped in before the colors faded—now I'm here." Blugwan stood and dusted himself off.

The Turul spoke again with a high-pitched chirp and a long trill.

"I think you are correct about that. Ordak is now determined to regain and extend his evil rule over the cosmos because of the Pixie. Today, in the Under World, it is peaceful for the first time in a thousand years—I wish it'd stay that way. The evil force is so dark and corrupt, it surfaces for no good reason—blasted Pixie!"

She turned her head, looking at Pewton, and her next question sounded like *kack, kack, kack.*

Blugwan turned his large head. "What? You're right. Absolutely! The Troll, Pewton. I had no idea he landed here. He must've gotten in the portal shortly after me. Just glad I didn't land right behind Ordak. The portal must have spat him out somewhere else. I'm sure he doesn't know we're here."

With another longer trill, Pewton stirred but lay unconscious. Blugwan said, "My, my. Pewton has the perseverance of a beaver. He knows the river's current is endless and harsh, but that never stops old Pewton from trudging forward to build something for himself. I guess he doesn't know that Trolls can only get so far in the Under World."

The Turul spoke with more of a chirp this time.

With quick laughter, Blugwan said, "You're not kidding. He's a good one to keep on our side."

With a longer and more serious message, this time from the Turul, Blugwan responded.

"Absolutely, if you say that Elias needs us, we're there! We must do what we can to help Elias and protect the Elixir of Life so Ordak cannot fulfill his evil plan."

The Troll began to stir and sat up with his eyes closed. He yawned and opened one eye and then another. He tried to speak, but nothing came out. He tried again, and this time, his voice was high-pitched and broken as he spoke. "Pewton thought he heard voices. Yes, and I see Pewton was right." Blugwan hollered with thunderous laughter.

"Welcome to the Isle of Eahta, my little friend—or enemy. Which is it today?"

"Friend. Pewton has learned. Oh, he has learned. For the first time, I questioned Hibush and asked why he would not use his powers for good, and he all but killed Pewton. I got to the portal, and it gobbled up Pewton and dumped me here. Let me help."

"My friend, you have been through a lot, and what you say is good, but you must win our trust. But I must say, you are worth the chance," said Blugwan.

Pewton stood up and puffed up his chest with his head held high. "Pewton will show Blugwan and you too, Turul—and Elias."

The Turul chirped and then tweeted.

"Very funny. Yes, very, very funny, my feathered friend. Okay, so what you're saying is that the best way to help Elias is for Pewton and me to be in the Temple when he arrives? You may be right, but I don't think I have to remind you, but we don't exactly blend into the crowd."

The Turul let out a short trill and ended with a chirp.

"Putting it that way, we'll do it. Right, Pewton?"

Pewton nodded as the Turul chirped more.

With a big grin, Blugwan leaned forward and clapped his large hands. "My, my Turul. Why didn't you say that in the first place? Since you are friends with the high Priestess of the Temple, show us the way."

11
Page Eight Hundred-Seventy
Day Three on the Isle of Eahta

Shin's secret room was octagon-shaped, and the walls were fifteen feet high. With no windows, it was lit by a source of light coming from pinhole-sized openings from the books that wallpapered every surface, including the ceiling. The strange room overflowed with books on shelves from the floor and curved to cover every inch of the ceiling. Defying the laws of physics, at first glance, Elias and Kelsa thought the ceiling was some kind of illusion, but it was no trick. There were shelves full of actual books that covered the ceiling. How the books stayed securely on those shelves was unexplainable, but on the Isle of Eahta, many things go unexplained.

On a table in the center of the room were more books, including page seventy-two of the book that the Turul delivered to Shin earlier that day. It was folded into a small square. The musty room, however, was tidy and orderly. Shin stood on a movable staircase propelled by two nods and a point of his chin. With a book in each hand, he crooked his neck and tilted his head to read the spine of another that was on a ceiling shelf.

"I've been meaning to develop a system. I don't have time for a system, but I need one. I'll find it—yes, I'll find it. The book is here somewhere," Shin said through his teeth as he was growing impatient with himself.

"You *do* have a lot of books, Shin," Kelsa said as she leaned against a shelf of large, old books. Pulling one off the dusty shelf, she bumped into the shelf behind her full of oversized and ancient tomes, almost knocking one to the floor. Because of her quick reflexes, she caught it before it hit the floor. She looked to see if anyone was paying attention, then turned her back and began to thumb through its yellowed pages. Oblivious to Kelsa's escapades, Elias sat at the table rubbing behind Cimbora's ears.

"You're a good boy, yes you are. Yes, yes, Cimbora, you're a good boy."

With his eyebrows nearly coming together, Shin peered down at Elias.

"What a good boy you are. You're my buddy, aren't you...aren't you?"

"Elias, I cannot concentrate. Would you mind keeping it down a teensy bit?"

Looking up, Elias said, "Oh, sorry. Sure. Boy, Shin, you *do* have a lot of books."

"Yes, yes, yes–so I've heard. Books have most of the answers to our questions, or they will offer us the path to find the answers on our own. But what you see here is just a fraction of my collection. There's more in the back." said Shin.

"You mean behind another hidden door?" Kelsa added as she blew the dust off one book.

"Oh no. Behind these books–on each shelf. They go much further back, and I always forget the spell that pulls the ones I want to come forward, as it is slightly different for each quadrant. Yes, I must take a

86

moment and come up with a system. Everything works better with a system. Yes, a system is needed."

Elias looked at the folded, torn-out page in front of him. He slowly opened the parchment as if he expected something to jump out. Turning it one way and then another, he tried to make sense of what he was looking at. It was some kind of colorful design, like a picture, and it took up the entire page. The image had three circles or rings within each other, and in the center was the shape of a flower. Four lines crisscrossed through the entire picture. At each endpoint of the four lines was the drawing of a monster-looking creature, but the colors throughout were vivid and beautiful.

"Shin, what is this a picture of?"

"Huh?" Looking down at Elias, Shin said, "Why, of course, that is the Temple and all that lays around its perimeter. It is very colorful, and it is called a mandala. It is a piece of art, but it also gives us a true picture of the Temple."

Elias scratched his head. "So, is this flower in the center of the Temple?"

"Yes, it is. It represents purity, growth, and renewal. The book I am searching for will tell us what is in each ring, or *trial*, that one must endure to be worthy to gain entry to the chamber where the Elixir is kept. This book I am searching for will describe the creatures that keep guard over the Elixir of Life in each ring and in the Temple. It's quite interesting, yes?"

"Yes. It's very interesting. What do you think, Elias?" asked Kelsa.

"I think I heard him say, 'trial that one must endure to be worthy to gain entry.' What exactly do you think he means?" Elias asked in a whisper.

Overhearing Elias' comment to Kelsa, Shin spoke up. "The traveler, who would be you, must successfully move through three trials to achieve or prove that you have the eminence required to handle, protect, or sip the Elixir."

Standing, Elias walked to one wall of books, folded his arms against his chest, and leaned against the shelves, "I'm pretty sure I need more details about each trial. So what are these trials all about?"

Pausing his search, Shin held the banister as he looked down at Elias. "Ah. Very good question. Very good question, indeed. Can you tell me?"

"What?" Elias craned his neck, and his eyes shot up to where Shin stood.

"Yes, what is a trial?"

"It is an obstacle...or test... or contest, a...," Elias answered.

"Precisely, Elias. One cannot reach the Elixir by sidestepping the trials. Each of the three achievements is necessary."

Throwing up his arms, walking back to the table, and slumping into the chair, Elias said, "You learn something every day. Zoltan didn't tell me about *trials*."

"It will be a cinch, Elias—that is, a cinch for you," said Kelsa.

Looking down at his amulet and pulling it away from his chest for closer inspection, Elias said, "Gosh, I hope so, Kelsa."

Kelsa pulled out another book and asked, "Shin, what is the title of the book you are looking for?"

"I'm looking for The Book of the Land that Doesn't Exist."

She closed the worn, leather cover of the book she had in her hand and mouthed the title. "Got it. Yep, I've got it," she said with a big grin.

"Hmmm. So that's where it's been hiding over these many island submersions, "he said as he began to zip down the staircase.

"Island submersions?" asked Elias.

"Without a way to record time, I recall points of my life by the number of times the Isle of Eahta dips into the sea, hence, 'island submersions.'"

"Hmmm—makes sense."

"Well, well, well. It was, literally speaking, right under my nose. Let's take a look as I believe it will have many—not all—but many of the answers Elias needs to continue his quest," he said, bounding down the last few steps of the staircase.

Shin, out of breath from rushing down the stairs, joined Elias at the table, and Kelsa joined them in the center of the room. She handed Shin the book, and before it was in front of him, he began flipping through the pages. Like lasers, his eyes seemed to burn through each word as he intently read and turned each page at a record pace. As he did, he would let out the sounds, *ahhh* or *a-ha*. Elias and Kelsa looked at each other, then at Shin, and then back at each other. Tight-lipped and bug-eyed, they said nothing but held in their laughter.

All beings are welcome to the Temple. All beings are not, however, worthy of partaking in the Elixir of Life. The essence of the Elixir must be cared for—must be valued—must be cherished—and must be preserved. As all humans have beliefs, when such beliefs lead to actions that create an imbalance, such as power, control, and greed, evil awaits an entrance for growth. CAUTION: The Elixir is not for such beings.

Earth and all the cosmos are in a state of equilibrium. Man is the only force that may imperil the balance as he is the only being that, at will, may disregard the Truths. The Truths are the Truths, and The Truths must stay balanced – wood feeds fire; fire created earth; earth bears metal; metal enriches water; water nourishes wood, and the cycle repeats and allows life to continue ad Infinium.

As many possess the gift—the Donum—those who may partake of the Elixir of Life are those who not only possess the Donum but those who possess the Donum who have been tested. Only then may the chamber open.

"Yeah, I know about that one already," Elias said, interrupting Shin.

The chamber may open to those who acknowledge the existence of the Two Powers. Good is the greater of the two, and evil is a relentless parasite. Understanding them allows for the extinguishing of one or both. Beware of those who say they understand them. If they understood them, they would reign supreme. Humanity chooses between love and fear, good and bad, and right and wrong. Though humanity may not understand why, humanity still chooses.

The world is connected in all ways. The Truths must stay in balance:

The power of the Endless Within comes from compassion. This balances the world. Cigam, the power that comes from this, may be used only for good.

Those who are worthy are those who see the rainbow of light and search for it in their darkest of hours. Although always present, not all see the Dancing Souls or the brightest lights in the cosmos, but it is they who are continually reaching for balance. Those who trust, believe, and most of all love will always see these lights and know and follow the direction it takes them.

"Wow. I'm not sure what all that means, but it sure sounds wonderful," Kelsa said, sitting back in her chair.

"Tas! That's all Tas." With a smile, Elias shook his head several times.

"What?" asked Kelsa.

"You are right, Elias," said Shin, "he wrote this book. I know you spent time with him at the Land that Doesn't Exist."

"Yeah, but he said he was some kind of caretaker of the place. He didn't say anything about the Elixir of Life. How would he know I would be here? Or did he? Zoltan didn't even know I'd be here until he made a split-second decision based on what he learned about Hibush and his plans to become the evil ruler of...of everything."

"Hey Elias," said Kelsa, "maybe he didn't know at that moment in time for certain, but maybe he had a hunch."

"Yeah, but who is he for real? I mean, he must be more than a 'caretaker' for some weird land...and that book is like 500 years old."

Shin slapped his palms on the table, and both Elias' and Kelsa's heads snapped in his direction. All was quiet except for a short bark from Cimbora, who was sitting at Elias' feet.

"Thank you," Shin said in a whisper. "My new friends, who Tas is and why and when he wrote this book matters not. What matters is that he has given us the information that Elias needs to ensure that the Elixir of Life does not get into the hands of Ordak. You will see as we plunge deeper into these words."

"Yeah, you're right, Shin," said Elias. Kelsa nodded her head.

"Thank you. Let's resume and look closer at these pages as we still need two things: a map and the code to unlock the chamber," said Shin.

"Ambrosia already helped with the first two. Eahta means 8 and 7 for the number of days before it sinks."

"Who is Ambrosia? "asked Kelsa.

"I met her on the beach before I started on the path here. She came here a long time ago and is one of the protectors of the Elixir. Isn't that right, Shin?"

"Yes, like me, we do all we can to protect the Elixir of Life."

Kelsa pulled the book in front of her as Shin stuck out his chin, nodded once, and winked. "I happen to like it when young people take charge."

As she flipped through the pages, she said, "I have an idea. Hmmm, nothing about unlocking the chamber on page 78." She then continued to flip through the pages. She turned to page 87. "This doesn't look right either. But let me see...oh yeah, page 870. Right here, it says, 'Unlocking the Chamber' right on the very top."

"How'd you come up with page 870?" Elias asked.

"We already know the first two numbers of the code– 8 and 7. I first flipped to page 78 and then 87 and thought I'd add a zero."

"Ahhhhh. Wise and intuitive. You are a very smart cookie—very smart." Shin said, leaning in. As Elias forced a smile and a quick shake of his head.

"Okay, *smart cookie*, what does it say?" Elias asked.

"Here it is," Kelsa said, using her index finger to read each word exactly how it was written.

Although there may be other ways to obtain the Elixir, there is but one way to unlock the chamber."

"Yep, sounds like Tas alright."

"I see. Yes, I think I understand," said Shin.

"You do?" asked Elias.

"Kelsa, keep reading."

Two numbers belong to the Isle of Eahta, and two belong to the rightful seeker of the Elixir.

"So, the other two numbers are important to you—just to you, Elias," Kelsa said as her words faded.

"What else does it say, Kelsa? I mean, does it give any other clues?" Elias asked.

Kelsa looked down at the page and scoured each word. She read a sentence or two aloud when she thought she was onto something but would end the sentence with a shake of her head. "Gosh, I don't see anything else."

Shin's bottom lip stuck out as he tapped his fingers on the table. He then spoke. "Elias?"

"Yes, Shin?"

Shin paused and spoke again. "Elias?"

Puzzled, Elias looked at Shin. "Yes, Shin."

"What prompted your journey? The very first time you ventured to an enchanted land."

"Nattymama told me that to find my answers, I had to go on a journey, and I should follow my heart as my heart will always lead me to who I truly am."

"Go on."

"And when you know this, your dream will be clear, and you follow your own path."

"Nattymama is wonderful," Shin said with a smile that puffed out his cheeks. "But as wonderful as she is and what she said, think further back. What caused you to seek her words of help?"

"Well, Papa told me that I had until my sixteenth birthday to decide how I would live my life—farmer, artist, or something else. He was pretty angry and didn't understand me. He told me that exactly forty days before my birthday. I remember it clearly as I shouted back at him—I was angry too—that I could make all those decisions in eight and a half weeks—forty days?"

"Ah. It sounds like these are the missing numbers. What do you think, *smart cookie*?"

"Yeah, they've got to be the numbers," she said.

"What? Shouldn't you be asking me?"

"Well?" Shin asked.

"Yeah, you're both right. So 7, 8, 16, and 40."

"It is your best bet, Elias. I do not relish telling you this, but while we were discussing this, we are now well into day three, and we still must figure out where you must go," Shin said as he rubbed his hands together and looked up to his many books."

Kelsa turned her head slightly one way and then another. "The third day? Why are we not tired—why don't we sleep?"

"Another good question. During these eight days on the Isle of Eahta, no one grows tired. It's just the opposite. This place is like no other."

"The powers here are a different sort of magic. It's...it's unexplainable," said Elias.

Shin spoke up. "Yes, they are, but life is unexplainable...the cosmos is unexplainable... our existence is unexplainable. Humans ask why and are always searching, and one day, those answers may come. But today is about a different search—*a different sort of magic*—and perhaps all we need is to examine this beautiful mandala as it will tell you how you may enter the Temple and what to expect. Day four is approaching. The other questions will have to wait."

12

The Moment Has Come

Elias pushed back from the table, stood, and walked to the other side of the room. Silent, preoccupied, and unfocused, he looked at the books inches from his face. Time was passing, and although time meant nothing on Eahta, he heard a loud tick of a clock in his head. That was real. He ran his fingers through his hair as it flopped into his face. Time may not mean anything here, but sinking into the sea and living here forever meant everything.

"Shin, I've got to get going, and I still don't know where I'm going."

"You're going to the Temple—to protect the Elixir of Life from Ordak," Shin said.

Turning his head sharply toward Shin with trembling hands, he said, "I know that. I don't know how to get there, and it may be too late. The three of us also need to get off this stupid island before it takes us down with it."

Everyone was motionless, and silence fell like an avalanche. Within a second or two, Cimbora poked up his head and gave out a nearly inaudible whimper. Kelsa went over to Elias and put her arm around his waist in a half hug but said nothing. In a monotone, Shin spoke up. "I understand. I will share with you all I know, and you will be on your way."

Elias forced a smile, and his shoulders relaxed. He realized he wasn't ready just yet. He and Kelsa went back to the table, sat next to each other, and faced Shin. "Shin, I am sorry. I just, I just...".

"Say no more, my friend. Let's get down to business."

Shin reached for the torn-out page that the Turul brought him and slid it in front of Elias and Kelsa. With his long, slender finger, he pointed to the very center of the drawing.

"This is where the Elixir of Life is located—this is the chamber. This is where you will use the numbers to unlock the door. The only way to protect the Elixir is for you to fend off intruders like Ordak. As long as it is not stolen or drunk by the wrong being at the last moment of the last day, you have done your job."

"So why does he have to unlock the door? Why not just stand in front of it when Ordak comes?" asked Kelsa.

"Very good observation—my, you are a *smart cookie*," Shin said as Elias rolled his eyes, and she looked at him through the corner of her eyes. "Here's why. If Ordak does not discover the passage there in time and the ground begins to tremble, you have done your job but must exit.

"Let's hope that happens, then we can just get out of there," said Kelsa.

"Yes, and you must make haste and get out of there right then. The only safe way out at that point is through the portal that is in the very chamber with the goblet and the Elixir. When you lift the goblet, the portal presents itself for a very short time—very, very short."

"That answers my question," said Kelsa.

"Does any of this become easier? I mean, whew!" Elias threw his head back, closed his eyes, and shook his head.

"Well, no," said Shin. "I'm sorry, Elias."

Elias grimaced. Kelsa put her arm around his shoulders. He smiled and motioned to Shin to keep talking. Shin reeled off all he knew to them as they soaked it in, like water to sandstone. He pointed to the four entrances and then at the three trials or rings that encircled the Temple. By the time he was finished answering their questions, Elias had more questions.

"So, let me make sure I have all this straight."

"Okay."

"I'm in good shape because I've got the requirements, so to speak, to be there?"

"Absolutely."

"And I've got the code to open the chamber?"

"Absolutely."

"We've got to pass through the portal when we feel the ground tremble?"

"Absolutely."

"And all I have is my dagger as a weapon?"

"Hmmm. You will have to be inventive. The dagger has some wonderful powers, as you are aware, but you will probably need more oomph."

"More what?" asked Kelsa.

"Oomph? All I need is more oomph?" Elias asked.

"The *best* word escapes me, but yes, you must be aware of the omens and seize every opportunity. The trials are grueling and will test the mind, body, and spirit. But be open to the Dancing Souls as they are behind you in your darkest hour. From it, you will pull from your Endless Within, and you will just know."

"So I will 'just know?'".

"Yes."

"Easier said than done," Elias said with a forced smile.

"You are more than what you think you are. You have already been tested. You have proven that you can do anything you set your mind to. It comes from *under* the amulet that hangs around your neck and thumps with the beat of your heart."

"I never asked for this, Shin."

Shin looked down, and the muscles in his face tightened, and his eyes welled up. "And I never asked to be forever on this island. As it is with every living soul, sometimes we must put aside, even for a moment, the life we have dreamed of meeting to embrace the life that has stepped up to meet us."

"I never asked to be whipped around the cosmos either, Elias," said Kelsa.

"Good points. Yeah, it's not about me—sorry. I was feeling sorry for myself."

"We all do from time to time. I don't blame you," said Kelsa.

"Thanks—both of you." Cimbora barked. "You too," Elias said, reaching down to scratch Cimbora behind his ears.

"You are a young man of humility—never lose that, but never lose sight that your power comes from within, and in your darkest hour, you have the brilliancy of the Dancing Souls behind you. The Dancing Souls are the good of all humanity for millions of years. Its light is brighter than a million of the brightest stars in the cosmos."

"And you've got me and Cimbora. We're with you all the way," said Kelsa.

"You're right about that." Elias reached out to hug Kelsa, and Cimbora's tail was a blur as he chimed in with a bark. Shin reached out to all of them and wrapped his arms around the two.

"Let's go," Elias said.

"Hold on, my dear friend. There's one more thing you should know," Shin said.

"Now what?" Elias said with a smile.

"I must tell you that the Temple knows who is approaching her. To navigate through the many obstacles and to confront the many beasts that protect the Elixir, your friends may be put in danger, for which you will have no power. We read it in the book. You are the only one who possesses the qualities necessary for this venture."

"Kelsa and Cimbora must go. This place will sink, and the three of us have to enter the portal."

"We're going," said Kelsa.

Shin stood up, walked around the table, stood behind them, and placed his hands on each of their shoulders. "I may be able to find another portal in one of these books." He slowly looked toward the ceiling.

"We don't have time. Besides, you said the Temple welcomes all, but only the chosen may sip from the cup," said Kelsa.

"Yes, I am sorry to say that we don't have much time. Yes, the Temple welcomes all. I just don't want anything to happen to you three. Knowing you for just a short time, I've grown so..., well, so attached, and this I speak from my heart."

"Oh, Shin! You are so sweet." Kelsa said.

With his face turning red, Shin motioned for the three to include Cimbora and join hands—or paws. "People enter and exit our lives as long as we live, some for a short time and others for a lifetime, but I will cherish this brief moment we had for the rest of my life."

"Shin, I will, too," said Elias. With her eyes tearing up, Kelsa nodded and hugged Shin. Cimbora nuzzled his head in and shared a bark.

Shin smiled. "I think it is risky, but I think the three of you must go. It is the only way, and you will find a way."

"It's settled. We're all going."

13
Approaching the Temple
Day Four on the Isle of Eahta

Like a scout and always twenty or thirty paces ahead, Cimbora led Elias and Kelsa deeper into the lush, green forest. Shin told them that the path that got them to the village would not lead them to the Temple. He told them to follow the little-known path directly behind his home that was rockier and the one that the vegetation to either side of the trail thinned out as they walked. When Shin told them that, they had no idea that the tall, thick, and wide blades of grass and the tall bamboo would shrink in half as they approached it. Shin said they would know they were on the right path when this happened.

"We're definitely on the right path, Elias. I mean, it's like the grass is actually telling us we're headed to the right place—weird."

Elias kept one eye on Cimbora and the other on the sky with hopes of spotting the Turul. Just then, a dragonfly landed on his hand. Elias paused, raised his hand close to his face, and smiled. The dragonfly flew away.

"Hey Elias, is that lightning in the distance?"

"Looks like it. It won't be long now," he said.

With his tongue hanging from one side of this mouth, Cimbora continued to forge ahead. Elias called up to Cimbora to slow down as he was sensing dangers could be lurking ahead. The lightning was fiercer, and the rumbles of thunder were more worrisome. Cimbora ignored Elias' pleas and seemed to trot faster.

"Hey boy, slow down. Slow down, Cimbora." The next thing they knew, he had vanished.

"Where do you think he is?" Kelsa asked.

"I don't know. He was on the path—we saw him. I think it takes a curve, so I bet he's up there but out of sight. Let's see what's up there, but we need to take it slowly."

With his dagger now in hand, Elias and Kelsa jogged up to the curve in the path, and as they turned the corner, they saw no trace of Cimbora.

"Where could he be?" asked Elias. "He was just here."

"Look, Elias," Kelsa screamed as she saw an imposing silhouette of a creature in the distance, and he was surrounded by bright red vapors. The figure looked like it could be a large man but was fuzzy around the bottom part of its body, so its legs seemed more like a cloud. Its long, spindly arms motioned for them to come closer.

"I...I don't know about that," said Kelsa.

"Yeah, I don't think so. Don't move."

The two stood still, and as they stared at the shadowy creature, Elias felt something press against his leg and jumped. "Ahhh! What is that?" It was Cimbora, and although Elias was relieved to see his friend, his body was tense, and he let out a big sigh. Kelsa let out a short nervous laugh, but a second later, she continued to lock her eyes on the phantom. Growling now, Cimbora reared back on his hind legs, and Elias did all he could to hold him back. With his powerful back legs, Cimbora's strength was too much for Elias, and Cimbora thrust forward, charging ahead. Only a few feet away from the red figure, Cimbora leaped to the creature, and as he did, he went through him. Both he and the phantom had vanished.

A cover of silence fell over the moment, and Elias and Kelsa stood frozen and awestruck at what they had just seen. Like a wave toppling a sandcastle, Elias crumbled to his knees and dropped his head. Silently, tears ran down his cheeks from his red eyes. Saying nothing, Kelsa kneeled next to him and wrapped her arm around his shoulders. In silence, Elias rose to his feet, and they walked a while, saying nothing until Elias spoke up. "Why, Kelsa, why?"

She looked at him, gave him a reassuring smile, and shook her head. She reached for his hand, but he pulled away.

"Thanks...sorry, Kelsa, but I'll be okay. I've got to believe he's okay. Cimbora is the most resilient, most intuitive, the most loving...he's got to be alright," he said, looking squarely into Kelsa's eyes.

"I'm sure he's fine and figuring out, right now, how to find us."

Elias smiled. "You always know what to say—and you are usually right. I'm lucky to have you as a friend."

Taking up most of their faces, they shared a big toothy grin and picked up their pace as they came closer to the Temple.

14
The First Trial

The green vegetation and large blades of thick grass, colorful trees and bamboo opened on top of a hilly expanse of endless blue and purple moss-like ground covering. With the forest behind them, they could now see in three directions. Kelsa pointed to the top of a mountain. "Look, Elias! That peak way over there is the Temple. It must be, even though it is too far in the distance to make it out very clearly. I can't really tell, but it's definitely tall and looks like it's on top of a big grassy hill. It doesn't seem like a mountain."

"Yeah, what's the big deal getting there? It shouldn't be too hard," Elias said, looking at Kelsa, hoping for reassurance.

"We've got this." Kelsa felt her stomach churning as it seemed a bit too easy.

They hiked in the direction of the Temple, and that brought them to an unexpected lip on the steep hill. Looking down, their jaws dropped simultaneously, and in shock, they looked at each other. Below them, they saw a wall of fire that must have been ten feet high, and it encircled the hill that the Temple stood upon. The flames seemed to need no fuel and were nearly all the same size. No smoke came from them, and Elias and Kelsa could begin to feel its heat.

"Shin—that Shin was so right," Elias said. "He said we'd encounter three rings of obstacles around the Temple—The Three Trials. Too bad he didn't tell us how to handle each one."

"Hey, you've got everything you need to get through there and the other two trials. But I'm now feeling a bit creeped out by this. Maybe I should go back to Shin and see if he has another portal for me to take. What if you can just skip through those flames, and I burn to a crisp—I don't have to tell you, but I'm not 'the chosen one.' I just don't know about this, Elias."

"What? You can't back out now. I mean, the portal is up there, and it's probably the only way out of here. Hey, you've been there for me, and I won't let you down. Besides, we're a team. We're in this together, and if you can't go through this safely, we will both turn back."

"I don't know about that Elias. I mean, we don't have any good choices right now.

Before Elias could say the next word, they felt the ground under them rumble. At first, they thought it was an earthquake, but this vibration was different. It got louder, and the rumbling under their feet didn't stop. They could not tell what direction the shaking and sound were coming from. Looking behind them, they saw a cloud of thick yellow dust.

"Let's run for it, Kelsa!"

"Okay—let's go!" They started to run down the hill toward the wall of fire as they had no choice. Charging toward them, they discovered it was a herd of Griffin in hot pursuit. With the body of a lion and the wings and head of a huge bird, these beasts were equally adept to the ground as they were to the air.

Out of breath, Elias and Kelsa had gone as far as they could as they were only a few feet in front of the wall of flames. The herd came to an abrupt stop and surrounded the two. A strange, raspy voice came from one of them.

"Seize the girl!"

Before they knew it, one of the Griffins grabbed Kelsa and took flight. The others followed. Within seconds, they covered the bright sunshine and flew toward the Temple. Elias felt his heart pound as if it would explode from his chest. His body was tense, and he screamed as loud as a clap of thunder. "My friends... my friends are gone. I should have known. They risked everything for me. And I'll risk everything for them. I WILL NOT let them down."

As if to meditate, Elias closed his eyes and thought. His muscles were limp, and he could see the red of the sun through his eyelids. He smelled a sweetness in the air as the dust quickly dissipated. He placed his palm over the amulet. The tension that ached each muscle melted away. He recalled the conversation he had mere hours before...,

"*Shin, you are being way too general. What are these three trials?*"

"*Oh, Elias, you are being, as you say, 'way' too specific. A trial for you is different from a trial for me...or for Kelsa". Looking down at Cimbora, he continued, "Or a trial for Cimbora.*"

"*You sound like Nattymama or Zoltan. Come to think about it, you sound like most of those I've met on my journeys.*"

"*Good. I hope you are right.*"

"*What? How come there is always more than one answer? Doesn't anyone have the answer?*"

"*It is for you to decide how you may overcome what it is you need to overcome. You have learned from many. You are ready for the next step in your life.*"

"*This is so unfair.*"

"*Oh? How so?*"

"I'm being called on to save the cosmos from all evil."

"Is that what you think? My, my. Elias, you are not saving the cosmos; you are saving yourself, and by doing so, you are saving the cosmos."

Elias opened his eyes and looked at the raging fire. He was hot, and sweat streamed from under his messy brown hair and dripped into the corners of his lips. He remembered what Tas told him: "Humans would do themselves a great service if they attempted to learn the world inside them before seizing the world beyond them."

He stepped up to the fire and thought of the *Secret of Fire* that Gaspar told him and that it is *the heart that tells you how close and how long. When you think about it, it has been too long. When something is precious, you must know how close and how long to expose it to what could destroy it. You feel it, you don't think it. Fire is an agent of change—both for good and for bad.*

Again, Elias put his palm over the amulet that hung from his neck, covered his heart, and whispered, "I believe in myself." Now, only six inches from the blistering flames, they separated and opened a threshold for Elias to pass through.

He journeyed on.

15
Ordak's Plan

Moments after Ordak faded from sight when he was confronted by Elias in Shin's home, he transfigured and reappeared as a Minotaur and stood in front of the Common House in the village. He felt weaker but knew that the island's powers were all he needed to restore his once-held dark powers and new forces he would bend and contort to make them part of his evil plan.

He entered the Common House to a huge room full of many bizarre creatures. Among the crowd were humans; according to their dress, they were lost in time from centuries long ago. Some were mingling and conversing with Minotaurs, such as himself, among other strange beasts and creatures. The humans preferred other humans, and the beasts enjoyed other beasts.

There were Fauns, who were half man and half goat and had the reputation of being peaceful creatures who seemed out of place with the likes of the others. There were Imps, who were fairies attracted to mischief and wanted to create havoc. There were Ghouls who fed on the death of those who perished. The Elves, who looked like tiny humans, were full of disease and hardship and were eager to spread what they had. Roaming freely were Gorgons who were beautiful but dangerous. Like strands of hair, their heads were made up of venomous snakes. Gorgons used their looks to deceive when they could. All these creatures and many others have something in common—they first came to the Isle of Eahta as mortal humans. What they had turned into may have had something to do with how they lived their life before their fateful trip that ended up on Eahta.

With this conglomeration of beings, there was an odd feeling of friendliness. They were telling jokes and laughing or howling, depending upon what kind of creature they were. There was an occasional tussle, but that never dampened the spirits of these beasts. Scanning the large room, Ordak was pleased as he knew he would fit in without being noticed. He felt he chose the correct likeness for his disguise.

"Well, well," said a Gorgon, "I believe this Minotaur is new to the House. I've never seen the likes of your ugly face."

"Yes, you are correct, Fawnia," shrieked a Ghoul, stepping forward. A small crowd was forming around them. "I make it my business to know who comes in and out of the House."

"Yes, I am new to Eahta."

"Can't be that 'new' as you didn't come here as a Minotaur."

"Oh?"

Those close by laughed hysterically as more gathered around.

"This Minotaur is hilarious," said Fawnia.

"Are you an ignoramus, or are you just trying to be funny—or both? You must have attempted to find the Elixir of Life."

"Oh yes, that's it, my attempt failed. Just being funny, but I failed."

"I would say you failed on both accounts." The crowd guffawed. "I'm not sure you're not an ignoramus, though. Let me put it this way...see those humans on the other side of the room?"

He turned and looked in all directions. "Yes."

"Well, they are all gutless, and we have very little to do with them. They were afraid to search for the Elixir, but we creatures dared to uncover it...yep, it takes some time to sink in, but that's why you are an ugly Minotaur. You failed just like us. But those of us who attempt and fail come back here to live FOREVER with powers we didn't have as humans. So we've become magical in a strange sort of way. Not the best trade-off, but some—make that most—didn't live to tell the tale." She turned and wrapped her long, thin arm around a Ghoul's neck. "But that's good for our close friends, the Ghouls." She laughed, and others joined in.

"Yes, you are right. It takes time for it to sink in. I failed—like you. So those on the other side of the room continue to live as humans?"

"They will live that way forever, all knowing they didn't even try to find the Elixir. Pity," said an Elf.

"Some of us are still determined to find a way to the Elixir. The powers it must have may be all we need. But the only way to get into the Temple is to be dropped in by the only creature who can do this," said Fawnia.

"Oh?"

"The Griffin, of course."

"There's our answer. We need to do this and correct this little misadventure," said Ordak. The place erupted into a sick laughter, and Ordak's anger grew.

"Oh, yes, we must 'correct this little misadventure.' You *are most definitely* an ignoramus. The Griffin are loyal to the Priestess who guards the Elixir," she said.

"Do they ever come in here?"

The crowd broke into even more laughter.

Fawnia shook her head, and the tiny snakes opened their mouths as she did, showing their fangs. "Let's give him a break on this one. I *do* know of one who comes in here from time to time, and for the right price, as we *all* have a price, he will do it."

"Oh? I see." Ordak said, raising his chin.

"It's your lucky day. He is here now—in the back room. He doesn't like large crowds."

"So all the Griffin wants, I'm sure, is to sip from the Elixir?" Ordak said, folding his huge arms across his wide chest.

"Yes, but that's not all. This particular Griffin wants to have a partner to make the world better...can you imagine that? He can't be tricked either. We've all tried. And that's why we will never hitch a ride on that Griffin."

"A partner for what? To make the world a better place?" Ordak said. He thought about this and then continued. "I like that idea. Can you make arrangements for me—I mean arrangements for this young man I know who just got here? He fits the bill. He wants nothing more than to make the world better."

"Hmmm. What's in it for me?"

"I will have, I mean, the young man will have all the powers of Eahta, and he will give you what you want. Don't worry; he and I are just about inseparable. He is desperate, and I am sure he will want this chance."

"Okay. Even if you are lying, we could use a little added entertainment around here. Get the kid now, and I'll get the Griffin—around back."

16
The Second Trial
Day Five on the Isle of Eahta

Only a few steps through the opening in the blazing wall, Elias heard a sound like the boom of a cannon and turned to see the fiery passageway had closed. Trying to make sense of what was now before him, he couldn't believe what he saw when he turned and looked back from where he came. The red and blue scorching wall from which he had just passed was now a sheet of blue-green water rolling down from nowhere and passing into nothing as the ground, miraculously, remained dry. A cool breeze was coming from it, and it gave his skin a tingle. *This place is bizarre— I like it! But I've got to keep going.*

Resuming his journey, he saw ahead a pitch black sky. The sky was full of rolling gray clouds stacked on top of each other. A trace of red and yellow outlined each cloud that, like a knife, helped cut into the darkness. Not too far in front of him, he saw another curving wall that he presumed was to protect the Temple from Elixir-robbing intruders. *Yep, that's the next Trial. Number two and counting. I hope another day hasn't passed—I don't know how long I've got—I can't keep up with it.*

The flashes in the colorless sky opened the boundaries of dark passages, leading to sinister existences that lay in wait for a time when the hollow hearts of some would be open. Elias knew the balance of forces and shear power were always precariously teetering on one tiny point. He decided it unwise to look very long at the flashes above him as he felt a tightening under where the amulet rested on his chest. He knew the sky was trying to tempt him to go another way. He kept his head down and moved forward.

From where he stood, the wall was gleaming and shining as twisted lightning bolts, like a knotted wire, struck the barrier in no particular pattern. He ran up to it and realized it was made up of clear gems. It was like glass, and the gems of different sizes were smooth. Looking down at the base, he saw it was littered with skulls and other bones. Constant bolts of lightning continued zipping through the sky and striking the wall of diamonds and other beautiful stones. Flashes of light filled the sky between each erratic bolt, and the echoing sounds from the clouds were like the roaring stampede of the Griffins he heard earlier. Without warning, the clamor momentarily turned into a loud, tumultuous sound and then faded to an odd silence.

"I should have paid closer attention to Shin. I just assumed I would have Kelsa by my side to help me figure all this out," he said as he looked for any clues of how to scale the wall without getting struck by lightning.

Distracted by the red and blue bolts striking the top of the wall, the thunder that came with each made him jump before he got used to the deafening and jarring sounds. Backing away from the wall, he thought it was best to keep some distance until he could figure out how to get beyond it. *Maybe there's a door or gate—or something I've missed.*

He walked with care, taking small steps as he examined the wall. He must have gone thirty yards before he stopped and looked at what appeared to be a solid wall with no hints of getting through it. His fists were clenched, and his body stiffened as he looked to its summit. He vented his frustration, screaming, "*WHAT DO I DO?*" He sat, slumped over on a boulder facing the wall, and between lightning strikes, the image of

Shin came to his mind. First, the images and his message were cloudy, but he began to remember exactly what he told him hours earlier.

"You will be confronted with a wall that appears to be indestructible—one of permanence. It is made of diamonds and special gems. Royalty over the Millennia has used this sparkling stone to command a sense of permeance, but we all know that what seems insurmountable allows for an opening that, at first, may not be so clear to us. What is impenetrable only presents a new way. Many souls have been lost to this Trial as they knew no way to overcome it. This ground is where these souls live in their death."

"So you are saying it's haunted?"

"Why yes, Elias, that sums it up very nicely."

"So, I picked up that you said it 'appears' to be indestructible and that 'what seems insurmountable allows for an opening that, at first, may not be so clear to us. What is impenetrable only presents a new way', so there is a way through it, right?"

"Ah, you are very observant, Elias. You must find its flaw...its crack...or perhaps the stone that is missing. Perhaps it's none of that. Perhaps it is in the way you approach it. Perhaps it is about the 'when'".

"Wait—what? Did you tell me how without telling me anything? So it's like finding a needle in a haystack."

"Precisely. Find that needle."

"Shin, I need more encouragement right about now."

"You will meet strangers here. Listen to them."

"You mean ghosts?

"They are the spirits of the wall. LISTEN to them."

Elias pulled out his dagger and used the tip to poke at the wall. *This is going to take forever, and I don't have 'forever,'* he thought, looking down and seeing the skulls at his feet. Taking a double take, he saw a figure of a woman over his left shoulder. She was walking up to him. She was not quite a giant, but she didn't seem to be like most folks he knew from his days in the village. Her hair hung to her ankles, and strands of her hair flowed as she seemed to glide toward him. Believing Shin was correct, this image didn't scare Elias, as he desperately hoped she might be able to help him. As she got close, Elias saw that only the glow around her made her appear larger than life.

"Poking around like that is futile." Just then, the lightning and thunder became more intense, and Elias' shoulders pointed up, and he twisted his head sharply to see the bolts striking just above his head on the top of the wall. The woman was unaffected by everything around them.

"That's what I thought, but I haven't got a clue."

"See these bones." She pointed with an open palm.

"Yeah, I don't want that to become me."

"No. No, you don't. They didn't listen. None of them. Most of them were men. Big burly men." She laughed and walked closer to Elias. "They pushed me aside. What could they learn from the likes of me?" she laughed with a snort and looked directly into Elias' eyes.

"I won't push you aside, I'll listen."

"I believe you. You do not seem to be like the others. I can tell such things as I saw these bones—most of them when they had flesh and hair and everything else. Oh, they knew better—ha!"

"So, how can you help me?"

"You can't go around it—it's a circle. You can't go through it—it is too thick with diamonds. Under it? No, as it is as deep and wide as it is high. So, you must go over it."

"What? That's like saying, 'strike me lightning—I'm right here.'"

With the most beautiful sound, she laughed and held her belly, and when she seemed to have no more laughter in her, she started up again. The various sounds of her laughter were like words.

"Don't all these bones belong to those who tried to go over it?"

"Young man, this is the time in the conversation that these bones pushed me away. "'We don't need you...what do you know?' They said the same thing as you. They didn't wait for the best part of what I wanted to tell them."

"Well, I want to know the best part. I won't push you away—really."

"Sometimes the answer is in the clouds," she said.

"Huh? In the clouds?"

"When you see the blue bolt followed by the red and that one followed by the yellow—go! Go! All other bolts are for show. They will not harm you, but by the time you count to twenty-seven, or is it seventy-two? Darn, which is it?" she said, pinching her chin. "Well, it's been so long since someone has listened to me and scaled the wall—correctly—that I just can't remember, but I'd go with twenty-seven."

"Ah, ah—not too reassuring,"

"No great reward is a sure thing. But sometimes, it is because we act—we do something—and that makes all the difference. We must prepare ourselves the best we can, yes? Do not hesitate—count and get over the wall before the blue, yellow, and red bolts come back."

Elias turned and looked at the wall. A dragonfly landed on one of the diamonds, jutting out of the wall. Surprised, he wondered how and why it was there. He noticed his breathing became a tinge faster and he felt his heartbeat under the amulet. He felt warm and calm, and he was clear-minded.

"Well, it's about twelve feet high, and I could use those diamonds sticking out and climb as fast as I can, and I should make it," he said, turning back to the spirit of the wall. As he did, she turned to sand, and morsels seemed to drop one by one and sparkled as bright as any stone in the wall.

"I believe her."

BOOM-CRACK-SHROOM! The entire sky glowed in long, staccato flashes and showed gruesome details to a sky that had probably never seen the sun. Elias slinked down and put his hand over his head.

"That wasn't it. Wrong color lighting. Okay, I'll be ready. When I see the blue bolt followed by the red and that one followed by the yellow, I'm going! Just got to count—just got to get over it. Twenty-seven seconds—no, I'm shooting to do it in twenty!"

As if he expected to see this triple threat immediately, he stood ready. He eyed the wall, looking for the right stones he could use to spring him to the top. But the wall looked like—a wall. It was flat. Sighing, he looked to one side, ran down to other areas of the wall, and stepped back, this time to survey more of the surface. As he examined the area, he focused in on a section, and he saw six large gems protruding in a pattern that looked like jug handles.

"That's it!"

The thunder stopped, and it was quiet and dark, but the gems still seemed to glow. He kept his eyes on the first few gems he planned to step up on and those higher up he would grab. Sweating but ready like the runner waiting to hear the fire of the gun, Elias touched the amulet and knew he could handle what was squarely in front of him.

Just then, out of the corner of his eye, he saw what looked like flickering candlelight coming his way. He turned and saw the same specks and more flickering light. They were Imps. Elias didn't know what they were, but they were coming into focus before his eyes, and they were small, horned creatures with sharp teeth and claws. They had long, bony tails that swung, and as they did, they gave off a spark. They had small wings, and some of them were flying awkwardly.

"Oh gosh. They *don't* look friendly. The lighting has got to strike soon, or I am going to be the supper for that pack of scabby pests."

Looking back and forth at each approaching line of Imps, Elias dripped in sweat and tried to dry his hands so he wouldn't slip when the blue, red, and yellow bolts lit up the sky. Within a second, there was the crash of a blue bolt, followed by the red and then the yellow. *One, two,* he counted in his head. The Imps were getting close, but Elias knew he would be only a memory to them by the time they managed to get close enough to cause a problem. Elias raced to the wall and jumped to plant his right foot on the first jug.

Five, six.

He reached up with his left hand, but his sweaty palm caused his hand to slip, and he fell to the ground on his back. In pain, he jumped up, pulled out his dagger, and swung it furiously around him as the Imps were at arm's reach. They backed off.

Nine, ten, eleven.

Reaching for the same stones as before, and without slipping this time, he was halfway up.

Fifteen, sixteen.

Next to his head flew an Imp, and with his dagger still in his other hand, he slashed it through the air, scaring away the intruder.

Eighteen, nineteen.

From below, the Imps used their tails to propel tiny flicks of fire that barraged Elias as he felt the burns on his arms, nearly causing him to lose his grip. His pain forced him to slow down his pace.

Twenty-one, twenty- two.

He began to question his next move. Knowing he would have to dig down and reach inside himself, he touched the amulet, and with that, he felt a new energy.

Twenty-four, twenty-five.

With his other hand, he reached to the top edge of the wall, and with that, he catapulted himself over it, not knowing where he would land.

In mid-air, he let out, "Twenty-seven!"

17

The Third Trial

Day Six on the Isle of Eahta

Cushioning his fall, he hit the surface of a body of water. He sank rapidly as the calm, clear water made way for a murky and muddy bottom. Stunned by the consequence of his leap, he had no time to inhale a deep breath, so it wasn't long before he felt his lungs searching for oxygen. Hitting the bottom, he was consumed by thick and sticky mud and sediment. Flailing to free himself and with all the energy he could muster, he lifted himself from the dark goo, and by stroking his arms and kicking his feet, he surfaced in no time. The tip of his nose first emerged as he huffed to pull in the air.

He reached out his arms to help him stay afloat as he kicked his legs to tread water and gain his bearing. His hair was matted to his face, and he swiped it to the side as he furiously turned in a circle, but he did not see the wall he had jumped from moments earlier. *Weird,* he thought.

The sky was azure, and the air was warm under the glowing yellow sun that was high above. He paddled over to the shore, and on his hands and knees, tired and weak, he crawled out of the lake. Rolling down into a rut in the sand that must have been made over time by the gentle waves that would lap the shore. Once on the shallow bottom, he spilled over on his back, and a breeze whipped through, giving him a shiver. Inhaling large breaths of air, his chest heaved up and down, trying to regain balance. The amulet rested on his chest and glimmered in the sunshine. After a moment of peace, he looked at his arms where he had been attacked by the Imps only moments earlier, and saw not one sore, scratch, or cut. His muscles throughout his body suddenly felt rested and at ease. Even his clothes seemed to be drying at a fast rate. *Weird...*

"I probably have a day left, if that," he said, sniffing and looking up and only seeing blue.

He sat up and pulled his knees to his chest, and at his eye level, he could see the water from which he had just emerged. Still a little shaken by the speed of his recent conflicting experiences, he rolled his neck and rubbed his eyes. Looking at his immediate surroundings and directly in front of him, all he could see was a curved shoreline of a serene and pure body of water that was covered with colorful lotus blossoms. It seemed there were more blossoms than water. Being a natural body of water, he thought, it was a perfect circle. Raising his head just a little more, what he saw was like a smack in the face. As if three giant lotus flowers were sitting on top of each other, it stood and was adorned with all the colors of the universe. It must have been twenty stories high. He jumped to his feet.

"So that's the Temple Eahta where the Elixir of Life is kept."

From the recesses of Elias' mind, Shin's voice was growing.

"You will know it when you see it. When the Temple emerges in front of you, you are on your own."

"I'm on my own?"

"Sorry if I was a bit unclear. Let me put it this way. Yes, when you see the Temple, you are on your own."

"Okay, okay...I get it."

Shin smiled and let out a slight chuckle. "My dear boy, very few have gotten to the Temple as it takes much more than human knowledge and calculations. One must possess attributes that are difficult to measure. When we move from our ordinary way of doing things to that of the Endless Within—or, putting it a bit differently—when we make the connection between our heart and our thoughts, we know we are not alone. When we need it, we are welcomed by the help of others. When we know this, we become smarter. We should be open to learning until the day we die, and those lessons come from those we know and those who step into our lives sometimes for, perhaps, just a moment. We all live with a ticking clock, whether we live on the Isle of Eahta, in the biggest city, or in a tiny cave. It matters not how many ticks we have left, but what we do with each tick of the clock that matters."

"So, I'm on my own and...I'm not on my own, huh? What I *do* know is that I need to get there—as the ticks of my clock are definitely running out," he said, talking to himself.

The sleepy and quiet waters suddenly awoke before him as a wave gently flowed up, creating a foamy wash on his feet. Another one followed—then they were rolling in faster and larger. He looked out and saw in the distance a rise in the water elevation careening toward him. He stepped forward and raised his palm to block the beams of sun to focus on the sparkling crest of water heading to the shore. He felt a warmness he had never felt before. It was as if the sun was warming him from the inside, and he felt at peace even though he did not know what was heading his way.

Atop the underwater current was speckled with colorful lotus flowers, gently and quietly rolling up and down. Now stepping back, Elias saw that whatever was forcing the water toward the shore had created a wave about six feet tall headed his way. He backed off even more. As the water splashed on the shore, a creature's head appeared through the white foam.

"What is that?" Elias was mesmerized by what was before him. It had the deep blue head of a large horse but with the tail of a dolphin. It blew a spray of water from its nostrils much like a seal, and he dried his long mane with three or four shakes of his head. Standing on his horse-like front legs with his tail slightly submerged but slapping back and forth on the water, Elias saw his first Hippocampus, which is known as a brave and powerful water animal. The blue creature seemed to tip his head to Elias, and he followed suit.

"You are the largest and bluest horse, if you are a horse, that I have ever seen. Hmmm, you seem friendly. You are definitely powerful—that's easy to tell."

The Hippocampus let out a neigh and then a snort or two. He turned his muscular and long neck to look back at the Temple in the distance and then back at Elias. He did it again...and again.

"Yeah, you *do* seem friendly. But are you trying to tell me something?"

The creature nodded as if he was answering Elias.

"Huh...maybe you are my only hope to get to the Temple."

Again, he turned his neck, looking at the Temple and then back at Elias.

"You understand me."

The Hippocampus neighed in response.

"Yep, you know what I am saying."

His blue friend nodded, turned, and faced the Temple. His tail continued to flop and slap the shallow water. Cautiously, Elias took short steps up to the creature and rubbed his surprisingly soft and smooth side with his warm hand. Still a bit unsure, Elias asked, "So, should I climb on your back? Would you take me to the Temple?" With his green, almond-shaped eyes, the Hippocampus looked into Elias' eyes. Elias couldn't help but smile as he knew the answer.

Elias slowly tried to mount him but found it difficult as the Hippocampus was so large. The formidable creature bent his front knees, and Elias used them as a step. He hopped on his back and scooted close to his head. Gently gripping his soft, long, luminous green mane, the

Hippocampus took off with a little warning. He swam with ferocious speed, keeping his head and upper body above the surface of the water for Elias' sake. Elias was bright-eyed, and his smile crossed his face as the wind took his long hair and whipped it in all directions. The spray covered Elias, and he couldn't help but taste a fresh sweetness coming from a mix of lotus blossoms and noticeably clean, pure air. As the Temple loomed larger as they came closer, Elias saw the full spectrum of colors swirl and dance all around him. He was full of laughter, and it just sprung out. As it did, his new friend laughed too—although it was different from Elias'—he knew he was sharing Elias' joy.

Once on the shore of the Temple, Elias hopped down and rubbed the side of the creature's large face. He looked into his eyes again and felt a connection that filled him with wonder. He had only learned about this blue 'horse' moments earlier, but from this powerful being came immense kindness and hope—something Elias always treasured throughout his young life, even when he didn't have the words to express it.

Before Elias took one step back, the Hippocampus bowed his head and turned, and all that was seen was the crest of a wave he created as he went further away in the clear, lotus-covered water.

18
Blugwan Opens the Threshold

Now, looking toward the Temple, Elias realized the enormity and splendor it possessed. His sense of joy turned into reverence as new questions flowed in and out of his head like the water he had just crossed. Raising the back of his hand to his forehead, he exhaled all the air from his lungs, ready to inhale a fresh breath to begin the last leg of his journey. Like all the journeys he had taken to this point, he knew nothing was a sure thing and that all he could do was put his best foot forward.

Making sure his dagger was still fastened to his boot, he reached to his chest and covered the amulet with his palm. He thought of when Nattymama had given it to him, and he remembered all those who had coaxed, cajoled, and tried to steal it from him. He thought of the times he wanted to give it away until he truly knew its meaning. Knowing he had little time left, he put all that aside and jogged closer to the Temple. He looked over his shoulder as he moved through the dense bush, mindful that all was not as it may seem and what was hidden below was where the truth sat.

Staying as quiet as he could, he approached the Temple, and he could see that it was surrounded by flowers. Some were larger than any he had ever seen before, and some were the size of his fingernail. The colors flowed harmoniously together, with some flowers displaying all the colors of the spectrum. Ancient trees strung from the flowerbeds and were covered with thick, twisting vines. Peering through the leaves and grasses, he saw one corner of what appeared to be a square, walled-in courtyard. From talks with Shin, he knew there were four entrances to the courtyard, with one at each arched corner. He could see only two. Above each arch were words with symbols: *wood feeds fire; fire created earth; earth bears metal; metal enriches water.* "Yep, everything is connected, and it is up to us to keep it in balance."

He saw a large beast that had the body of a man and the head of a bull guarding each gate. This Minotaur had his large muscular arms folded across his chest and had a shiny, wide-tipped blade in one hand pointed to the sky.

Letting out a sigh, he said, "Good grief, now I've got to get past that guy? He's huge! I don't want to cross that guy—he seems mean." He studied the guard closer, and a big grin came across Elias' face. "Oh wow! Is that? It can't be. Is that who I think it is? I just don't remember that tattoo on his arm. Hmmm. Well, there's one way to find out."

Making sure the Minotaur could not see him, Elias yelled, "BLUGWAN," and ducked down and out of sight.

The Minotaur looked one way and then another, "Elias, is that you?" he said just above a whisper. "It's safe to come out."

Elias popped his head up from his hidden spot. Blugwan waved his massive hand, and Elias ran and jumped into his friend's mammoth arms.

"Elias, how did you know to come to *this* entrance? My entrance?"

"The blue horse of the lake brought me here."

"Ah, yes, I know him, and that answers my question. His name is Cerulean."

"Perfect fit...he got me here in no time. I wasn't sure if you were *you* or not. Is that a new tat?"

"Thanks for noticing," he said almost in a shy manner.

"A huge lightning bolt—perfect."

"I thought so. I mean, after what we went through."

"Blugwan, I'd love to stay and chat, but I've got to work fast—I mean, the eighth day is almost here. But first, do you know if Kelsa and Cimbora are safe?"

"I am sorry to say that I do not know, Elias," he said, slumping his mighty shoulders.

With a big sigh and looking away, Elias said, "Okay. They are not new to this game, so I am sure they will be here soon. They've just got to be okay. In fact, I know they are."

Nodding his head, Blugwan reassured Elias, "I know you are right—I just know it. How did they go missing?"

"Cimbora was taken by a creature that was surrounded by bright red vapors. It looked like it could be a large man, but its legs seemed more like a cloud... and Kelsa was captured by a Griffin. They came charging at us from nowhere, grabbed her, and flew away."

Blugwan smiled and stood straight, "Elias, I think Kelsa must be in the Temple."

"What do you mean?"

"Griffins protect the Priestess and the Temple. They are her army."

"So, they purposely sought her out and captured her—but why?"

"Not sure, but one thing I know for sure is that this journey can only be taken by one person. Knowing this, maybe they lent you, and them, a hand—do you know what I mean?"

"Yeah, Blugwan, that makes sense—wow, makes me feel good."

"But I don't know anything about Cimbora. That creature you described is something I've never seen. It seems more like someone was disguised... or worse, under an enchantment."

"You don't think it could've been Ordak."

"I don't think so. He has no use for Cimbora.

"Oh? Why?"

"Ordak is weak—yes, he is gaining powers, but he's focusing his powers on getting to the Elixir and not coming up with a bargaining chip. Not enough time for all that."

"You're probably right, Blugwan. At least, I hope you are. But I am prepared for whatever he throws at me."

"That's the spirit, Elias. Oh, there's one more thing you need to know. Pewton is hidden in the Temple somewhere."

"What?" Elias stepped back and looked squarely at Blugwan.

"Before you get angry, Pewton has changed. He wants to help—believe me."

"I don't know, Blugwan. That Troll has caused all of us a lot of problems from the first time I saw him."

"I know, I know. If he does anything, I will have your back."

"I know that."

"You must go, and I won't be too far behind you. You may need backup. Elias, there is no more time for talk. You must get to the very top of the Temple to find the Elixir of Life. Once anyone crosses this threshold into the courtyard," Blugwan pointed to the opening with his enormous hands, "they are welcomed."

"Welcomed?"

"If a being has entered the Temple through one of these four gates, they are welcomed to the Temple. But this doesn't mean they are entitled to The Elixir. One must have successfully passed through the Three Trials to be worthy of The Elixir of Life. Just making sure you know that."

"Well, been there, done that! But how do you know all this, Blugwan?"

"When you're at one of only four entrances—and exits, you hear a lot of things. Go, Elias, go. More will be revealed to you by the women who are the guardians of the Elixir. You will meet the Priestess. I have no more information to tell you.

Elias nodded and crossed the threshold.

19
The Temple
Day Seven on the Isle of Eahta

Racing through the entrance, Elias found himself in a courtyard paved in white marble stone and outlined with pristine but colorful gardens. There was a stream running close by and flowing into the Temple through a round, highly decorated framed aqueduct. He saw many stone benches throughout the courtyard and next to the stream. It made him think of his Nattymama as she would sit on her bench watching the bubbling water cascade over stones and meditate at the end of the day. It was important to her as it reminded her that life is sustained by water, and it ensures our future. She would tell Elias, "Keep looking at the water as it flows. The water knows what it needs to do."

There was a crisp, sweet scent in the air due in part to the variety of plants and flowers that filled the space. Mixed in with the vegetation, the area attracted the occasional finch, sparrow, or cardinal that would interrupt the silence with their song. There were no people that he could see. It was peaceful, but that abruptly came to an end.

A tall woman with a long flowing robe appeared from nowhere and startled Elias.

"Hello, Elias. We've been expecting you."

He turned to her and felt a wave of panic. "What? You have? Oh, yeah, I guess I should be used to that by now." His moment of anxiety melted away.

She turned her head to one side and then raised her gaze to the sky. "These skies are clear and hide nothing; it is peaceful here. Do you like it here, Elias?"

"Well, yes—and no. Getting here was all but clear and peaceful, and now that I am here, in this courtyard, I haven't had time to soak it all in. See, I have very little time to make sure that the Elixir of Life stays out of the hands of Ordak."

"Yes, Ordak. We know he's coming, too. He has yet to show his face within the courtyard. We will help you with your task."

"We? There are others?"

"Yes, Elias. I am one of many Priestesses that serve as guardians of the Elixir."

"No men?"

She smiled. "No, Elias. Men seem to be the vast majority who come here to take the Elixir, but only a few over the millennia have come to protect it. You are among those few."

"Do you know Zoltan?"

"Yes, he has been here many times to protect the Elixir."

"He has?"

"Yes, we know him well,"

"How about Shin? Do you know him?"

"Yes, Shin speaks the truth and helps all those who seek the truth."

"How about Tas?"

The Priestess quietly laughed. "My, you have many questions. And yes, we all know Tas."

"Hmmm. It's all coming together for me now."

"Elias, before we go in, I will tell you that there are two beings inside who claim they will help you, Kelsa and a Troll named Pewton."

"Whew! I am so glad to know that Kelsa is okay—and Pewton, too. What about Cimbora, my dog? Is he here?"

"I cannot say I have seen any dogs around here for a long time."

Elias looked down. "He'll be here. I just know it."

"I'm sure you are right, Elias. As far as the other two, I am happy to hear that you know of them. They did not come here in the traditional manner, but they may help you. Because they did not travel through each Trial, they are not in the position to defend the Elixir – only you, Elias."

"Is it possible for Ordak to come the way I came?"

The Priestess stepped closer to Elias, and as she towered over him, she gently looked down at him. "It is impossible for him to have successfully come the same way as you. The cunning, the ruthless, and the evil, however, find ways. They *find* ways. They are an unfortunate disease on the soul of mortals. What destroys mortals is themselves. Yes, Ordak can steal the Elixir, and we do whatever we can to protect it. Will you please follow me?"

They walked in a counterclockwise direction around the Temple until they found a long and wide staircase leading up to a magnificent entry. As they climbed the stairs, the Priestess told Elias that every nine steps represent each day that the Isle of Eahta lives up on the surface of the sea.

"But why nine stairs?"

"Very good question. The number nine is the last single digit, but it is the greatest in value of those that come before it, so because of this, it represents wisdom and experience... generosity, giving, loving, and compassion. This number is about *endings* but opens a door for *beginnings,* and there is great energy in where we begin and where we end."

"I see. I'm not so good at math."

She paused with a smile and looked at Elías. "No need to worry about math. It is whether you know its significance or not and if you possess the attributes I spoke of. But Elias, it is a never-ending journey of renewal—life, that is. Anything alive looks for renewal."

With a sense of urgency, Elias stepped through the entrance before the Priestess. Only a few steps into the cavernous, circular room, Elias was awestruck and felt small and powerless. Sighing and shaking his head, he felt the tension throughout his body. The gigantic room was adorned in white marble, but colorful murals hung throughout. It had a circular staircase around the perimeter to the very pinnacle of the Temple. Sunlight poured into the structure from all points but was most radiant from the very tip of the lotus bud-shaped Temple. He turned to the Priestess, but she had vanished. Alone, he stepped further into the room when he heard the resonant clanging sound of a mallet pounding a massive gong. He looked in all directions but could not see where the sound came from. Each time the gong was struck, the echo took a dozen seconds to fade away.

SHA-BOOONG

SHA-BOOONG

SHA-BOOONG

SHA-BOOONG

SHA-BOOONG

SHA-BOOONG

SHA-BOOONG

Then, it was silent.

"Seven. It's day seven," Elias said, running to the base of the circular stairs. He climbed the staircase, taking two steps at a time. Stopping once halfway up to catch his breath, he looked down and saw the many faces of the women who were the guardians of the Elixir. This inspired him to continue at full speed to the top of the Temple.

Arriving at the pinnacle, the room was open and large. He saw in one direction the vastness of the sea and its endless white caps as far as his eyes could take him. He walked out to an expansive balcony, and beneath where he stood was a rocky and jagged beach being thrashed by gigantic waves the size of tall buildings he had seen in Budapest. *Ah, so that's the rocky coast Ambrosia told me about. No wonder why their boats were wrecked,* he thought.

In the opposite direction was a similar balcony that overlooked the Isle of Eahta. He could almost retrace his steps, looking out to the lush, green land he had just traveled. Much to his bewilderment, the other two directions were foggy with peaks of stone pillars that thrust through the clouds. It didn't make sense. How could this be? Elias always looked at what was new to him with fresh eyes.

Knowing time was precious, he knew he had to find the chamber where the Elixir was kept. "It must be in this curved wall." In the center of the room was a circular wall or a cylinder-shaped room with cracks running through it. Upon closer inspection, he thought some of the cracks might be the outline of a hidden door. Looking closely at the maze of lines and cracks, he ran his palm over them. As he did, he heard barking in the distance. "Cimbora! Is that you?" The bark was now louder. Elias turned and saw Cimbora at the top of the long circular staircase.

With a grin that covered his face, Elias squatted down with outstretched arms. At full speed, Cimbora ran and pounced on him, licking his face as fast as he could. Knowing that time was running out, Elias calmed his friend and looked him in the eyes. "So, boy, you okay?"

Cimbora barked.

"So you're saying that red glowing figure was Zoltan? Ah-ha. Zoltan still has many tricks up his sleeve—always looking out for us. Cimbora, we've got to find Kelsa and Pewton and secure the Elixir before Ordak gets here. Even though time doesn't exist here, I say we need to act fast no matter what—hold it! I just understood every bark like you were speaking my language...I can finally talk to *and* completely understand you. This is awesome."

Cimbora trotted up to the wall and sniffed at the cracked surface. He walked around the perimeter of the massive circular room and paused. He reared back and barked several times.

"Ah, good boy." Elias felt around the cracks and merely pressed in on one side, and a hidden door opened. Kelsa rushed out and into the arms of Elias. With a swooshing noise, the door closed behind her.

"It's about time. It seemed like I was in there forever."

"Sorry, I got here as fast as I could. I *did* have a few *Trials* to get through—anyway, the door was unlocked. I just pressed it, and it opened."

"Hmmm. Well, it was locked from the inside." Kelsa stood straight and folded her arms.

"Uh-huh, I see, "Elias said with a chuckle.

Kelsa slugged Elias on his arm. "Yes, Elias, it was bolted shut."

"Ow!" Elias blurted, rubbing his arm. "I believe you; just don't hit me again. You're worse than the Imps I ran into. That reminds me, have you seen Pewton?"

"What? Who?"

"Yeah, Blugwan said he was here and would help—he's changed. That's what he said."

With her hands on her hips, Kelsa spoke up, "Oh, really? No, I haven't seen him. Wait a minute. You saw Blugwan?"

"Yeah, he and Pewton are here. Blugwan was guarding one of the entrances to the Temple. He's got our back."

"I hope Pewton does too."

"Like I said, Blugwan said he's changed."

"Let's hope so. Maybe he's behind one of these other doors too."

They looked around the wall of the circular room; all the cracks faded, and the wall was solid. Elias' brow squinched together, and he looked at Kelsa as she lifted her palms and shook her head. Cimbora barked and began to sniff the wall again.

"He'll show up if he's here, but we need to get to work and find the Elixir before Ordak finds his way here," Elias said.

20
Ordak Drops In

Ordak's nefarious plan to trick the Griffin seemed foolproof. He would transform to look like Elias and say all the right things to win over the Griffin. Looking awkward and unnatural, he waited for the Griffin. When he finally arrived, the Griffin started right away with his interrogation.

"So, young man, are you ready to make the existence of all beings better?"

Ordak paused as the very thought of this question curdled his cold blood. "Of course. I want to take the Elixir and share it with all so that everyone has the chance for a better existence on this planet," he said, looking to the ground and feeling good about what he had rehearsed to say.

"I see. Do you have the answer to open the chamber where the Elixir is kept?"

"Huh? Oh yes, the answer. I have them." Ordak didn't know what to do with his hands and couldn't think of how a sixteen-year-old mortal boy would act. He rolled them around, and he kept moving his fingers.

"Look at me when we're talking."

"Of course." Ordak looked up at the Griffin, but this unnerved him even more, and one of his eyes twitched.

The Griffin took a step closer to Ordak. "You know it's not just sitting in the Temple for anyone to step up to and partake?"

"I know that. I am not a fool." Ordak was tense, and his voice became louder.

"So angry for a young man who wishes to do good."

Cooling down quickly, Ordak said, "Oh, I am not angry. I am of a serious nature, and I am focused on my responsibility. Are you or are you not going to help me?"

The Griffin paused, looked around, and stuck his face right in front of Ordak's. "I will help you, and we will make a deal. I will deliver you to the Temple, you will acquire the Elixir, and then meet me at the entrance of the Temple. This way, we may share the Elixir as partners so that we may make the lives of others better. Do we have a deal?"

Ordak grinned. "Oh yes, Griffin, we have a deal."

"I'm risking my life for you, Elias. As a Griffin, I am loyal to my mission: to protect the Temple, the Priestesses, and the Elixir of Life. But I also know it does no good unless the Elixir helps to better the existence of all beings. Today, and for a millennium, it sits idle to no one's benefit except a precious few."

"Yes indeed. I agree with you wholeheartedly. You are absolutely on the mark."

"Hmmm, there's something about you that seems—odd. You speak differently from what I remember teenage boys to sound like," said the Griffin.

"Ah, ah, I am precocious, yes, that's why," he said with a blank look on his face.

"Funny, but I had already ruled that out. Let's just drop it—are you ready?"

◆ ◆ ◆

They flew over the colorful, dense forest. Ordak held tight around the Griffin's large neck. Now that his plan was hatched, he knew that once in the Temple, he could get his hands on the Elixir—but how? He knew he had to conserve his powers as it may take all he could gather to force his way through the Chamber door, drink from the goblet, and open a portal to escape. He knew his aim in life may come to an end without successfully obtaining the Elixir and doing so without many distractions. Evil, fear, disaster, and every ill known to all living creatures depend on his success. He must live forever.

Soaring high above the Isle of Eahta, they could see for miles. In the distance, they saw the wall of fire. Ordak knew this was the First Trial and was pleased that they would soon be passing over it. To Ordak's surprise, as the Griffin approached the wall of fire, he descended and landed twenty-five feet in front of it.

"What are you doing, fool? *I mean, friend?*"

"Even a Griffin needs a rest, especially when carrying a passenger. You may be precocious, but you need to work on how you speak to others. You're beginning to wear thin."

"I apologize. Yes, please rest, but please understand that I'm just in a hurry as I must find the Elixir before the island sinks into the sea. My nerves are getting the best of me. That's all."

"Do not worry; I am fully aware of this, *Elias.* I am just happy to have finally found a partner."

The wall of fire raged, and Ordak looked at it intensely, thinking he could find a way to get beyond it without having the annoying Griffin around any longer. He had enough of his companion.

"So, is the only way to get beyond this fire is over it?"

"No, Elias, but that is how I will take you. Only certain beings with certain attributes may go the other way."

"And what way is that?" he asked with sarcasm in his voice.

"Through it, of course. It opens. Your questions give me cause to wonder about you. How did you get to Eahta anyway? Now, thinking about it, I usually hear about new guests to the island."

"Ah, ah...since time is so precious, let's not talk about mere details like that. Let's just go over the wall of fire when you're ready."

Ordak mounted the Griffin, and they took off over the wall of fire.

◆ ◆ ◆

Just over the wall of fire, the Griffin was flying close to the ground and getting ready to land again. "Why are you stopping again so soon?"

"Do you not see that wall of diamonds and the bolts of lightning coming from the black sky and striking it at will? I would prefer not to be struck today—how about you, Elias?"

"I see. What is the plan?"

"I have done this hundreds of times before. I will wait for the right time."

Ordak was growing impatient. He was slowly getting more of his dark powers back and tried to control the Griffin's mind with a spell, but it didn't work. He had used the powers he acquired from Hibush to transfigure several times as he waited for the regenerative energy from the island to fully kick in. But now, running out of time, he desperately needed it before he could attempt to confront Elias and seize the Elixir to gain all the riches he thought he deserved. This frustrated him even more. Out of frustration, he blurted, "When will I get my powers back?"

"You ask when you will get your powers *back*? What powers do you speak of?"

Ordak said nothing, and the Griffin did not press for an answer. He didn't need an answer from Ordak as he now knew what he had to do.

Once they were over the wall of diamonds, they could see the Temple.

"Isn't it beautiful?" said the Griffin.

Ordak sighed and, without attempting to hide his true feelings, said in a monotone, "Yeah, yeah, yeah. It's beautiful."

"Elias, the shore is still perhaps a mile away or so, but I will drop you in this pure body of water, and you will swim the rest of the way."

With his throat closing, Ordak felt betrayed and shouted, "What? You will do no such thing?" Like a vice grip, Ordak grabbed the neck of the Griffin and uttered a vexing spell to change the Griffin's mind, but it was too late. The Griffin began to fly erratically, causing Ordak to lose his grip on the Griffin's neck and his concentration on the spell he was conjuring up.

"Sink or swim whoever you are," and with that, the Griffin whipped in zigzags, dumping Ordak into the water below.

Exhausted and with any resemblance to Elias having been washed away, Ordak managed to swim to the shore. Face down in the sand, he pulled himself up and cursed the Griffin, who taunted him as he circled above. Turning his focus to the Temple, he pulled himself up and began trudging toward it.

21
The Chamber

Using the palms of both hands, Elias and Kelsa began to run them over the now smooth surface of the rounded wall that, moments earlier, held a door from which she emerged. There were no cracks, seams, or openings of any kind; neither could detect anything that yielded a clue. Cimbora sniffed where the floor met the wall and continued circling the large room in the middle of the larger one until he was out of sight.

"Kelsa, if the door to the chamber is up here, it's got to be in this wall."

Kelsa looked in one direction and then another. "Yeah, it is dead center, and all around us is open space. I don't get it."

Elias looked to the floor while pacing back and forth. "So what was the room like that you were in? Maybe that will give us something to go on. I mean, did it have other doors that you could tell?"

"Just the one that you *unlocked* and pushed open. It was a large room with chairs. No windows, but it was bright. It seemed like I was there forever, but I really wasn't in there too long. A Griffin told me you would be at the Temple soon, and he knew you'd be up here to find me."

Only half listening, Elias said, "Hmmm, this is really strange...I mean, we all saw the outline of the doors disappear."

"That's it!"

"What? What's it?" Elias asked anxiously.

"The code will make the door appear."

"The code will make the door appear—hmmm, I think you may be right. I just figured we'd see *the* door to the chamber. But nah, it's too obvious now that I think about it. You're probably right; I just need to say the code—but remember, he said I had to push something while saying it. I think that's when he told us about the triangles."

"Right, the triangles are key to all this, "said Kelsa.

Just then, they heard Cimbora bark from the other side of the cylindrical room. They ran around to see what he had found. He was standing on his hind legs with his front paws scratching at what looked like a hundred points of all kinds of triangles coming together at the center of the wall. Like a mural, the surface was high and wide, and it was full of triangles. Mouths open, Elias and Kelsa stared at the huge, curved wall with thousands of lines all intersecting and forming hundreds of angles.

"That wasn't there three minutes ago...so, what did Shin say about all these triangles again? I mean, look at all of them," said Elias, pointing to one and then the next.

"Don't worry Elias, he said, '*when you see the six distinct shapes of the triangle come together in a point, that is the core of the cosmos. All things come from this point, and all things must return to this point.*'"

"Yeah, and I am counting on you as I am crummy in math. But he also said that the triangles must be the six distinct triangle shapes—the isosceles, equilateral, scalene, the... the acute, the right and the...and the... obtuse." Elias stuck out his chin and nodded once.

"We've got to find these six and the point they all touch. That's where you push and say the code."

They scanned the wall, and it appeared to them to be just a jumble of lines. Both were getting frustrated, and with a sigh from Kelsa, they turned to each other.

"Let's stand back, and maybe we will see it – like a constellation in the sky," said Elias.

They stood, backed up, as they continued to scan the wall. Looking one way and then another, they would find four unique triangles, but the others were the same—or some similar variation. Cimbora barked, bolted to the wall, and stuck his big wet nose on the correct formation.

"Way to go, buddy. We just needed to look from a dog's eye view," Elias said.

"Okay, so what's the code? Seven and eight from the island, and your numbers are forty and sixteen."

"Yep. Let's give it a try." Just then, they heard a rumble sounding like long rolling thunder, and they felt the floor tremble slightly. "We don't have much time, but I think we're going to make it before Ordak gets here. I just know it," Elias said.

Elias pushed the tip of his index finger to the exact center of where the angles came together and recited the four numbers. Nothing happened. Then, he recited them backward and tried mixing them up in different sequences. Shaking his head, he looked at Kelsa.

"I know—add them together," Kelsa said.

"Good idea—so forty and sixteen is, ah, ah."

"It's seventy-one. They all add up to seventy-one."

"Thanks, *smart cookie.*"

Elias tried the number, but again, nothing worked. This time, the rumble was longer and louder, and the floor shook. As quickly as it came, it ceased, but not before it bounced them to the floor.

Sitting on the floor, they talked it out. "What were your two numbers again—from what?"

"Papa gave me forty days to make up my mind to be an artist or what he wanted me to be—a farmer. And that landed right smack on my birthday when I turned sixteen. So—forty and sixteen."

"Hmmm, I think I know the problem. When you turn sixteen, it is actually your *seventeenth* birthday. It's got to be seventy-two—not seventy-one!

Elias bounced up and, again, pressed the tip of his finger where the angles converged. Slowly but with boldness, he said *seventy-two*.

A moment passed and–nothing. They both frowned, but before they could say a word, they heard stone sliding on stone, and then it was strangely quiet. A moment later, a door in the shape of a star materialized before their eyes. It began to open with a radiant light behind it. As it opened, a bright light came from behind them and filled the space. They instantly turned to see what was causing the light. Elias' eyes grew large. "I can't believe it?"

"Who is she?"

"Ambrosia? Is that you?" asked Elias.

"Yes, Elias, I am the High Priestess—the keeper of the Elixir of Life."

"What? I thought you met her at the beach sitting in the sand." Kelsa said.

Elias looked at Kelsa and nodded his head, "Yeah, I didn't know she was the High Priestess of the Temple. I didn't know she'd be here." He turned to Ambrosia and said, "But... but you knew I was looking for the Elixir to protect it and..."

"And what, Elias? I set you off on your journey, didn't I? Your journey and the many feats you accomplished have made you worthy to protect the Elixir. Not the Elias I met on the beach. It was the only way."

She approached the opening and extended her hand in a gesture for them to enter the room. It was a large area with four streams of water coming from different directions and emptying into a large clear pool. A lone gold goblet stood on a pedestal to one side. It was adorned with many diamonds and designs of fire, earth, water, and trees. A wood fire burned continuously to one side.

"So, it's ...*water*? The Elixir is water?" Elias asked.

"Yes. It is the purest of all waters. The Elixir comes from four sources on the planet, and when those sources merge, it strengthens the most vital of all liquids in the cosmos. As such, it must be safeguarded. Without it, the land becomes barren, and all living creatures, from insects, animals, and humans, will perish throughout the world. This is why we must protect what gives us life, has given us life for millions of years, and may give us life for millions more. With it, the planet lives forever. Nothing, *nothing* can replace it—thus the Elixir of Life."

Puzzled, Elias looked to Kelsa and then back at Ambrosia, "I thought the Elixir of Life gave someone who drank it eternal life, and that's why Ordak wants it—just like Killybegs and all the others who risked their lives to find it."

Ambrosia directed them to a stone bench, and they sat. "My young friends, stories grow, wishful thinking, desperate minds, rumors, lies, and deceit; most times, it is to make a fortune. Beings with intellects—humans—tend to look for the easy way out, but there is no easy way. They search, conjure, and fabricate tonics, potions, powders, and elixirs to give them something for which they overlook—the present moment. Ironically, their quest for eternal youth only wipes away their youth—the same youth that they so desired to capture in a bottle. They focus on what was and what may be but overlook the only time that matters, and that is *now*."

"So Ordak *only thinks* the Elixir of Life will give him a million years of an evil reign?"

"Happily, my answer is yes. He has already lived a thousand years, as evil is not a person; it is the absence of love— it is fear. If humans let fear into their hearts, evil lives and may live forever."

Feeling a bit shaky, Kelsa spoke up, "So if he finds out, what will he do, Ambrosia?"

"There is no telling, but my guess is that he will most certainly contaminate it for the billions of life forms on this planet. His hideous discontent and failure will enrage him so that his last deed will be to bring all living beings to their knees. It's hard for me to believe anything else."

Elias reached down to pet Cimbora on his head, and Kelsa squatted down to rub his side. They were trying desperately to absorb what they just learned. Ambrosia walked to the balcony that overlooked the rough sea. "You are doing the right thing. Rest assured, Elias, there is no magic strong enough to create an Elixir that gives one being eternal youth." She turned and looked Elias in the eyes. "But Elias, there is one Elixir that gives the living all the life they should have and safeguards their future. Water is alive. It feeds our body, our soul, and our mind. If we take care of it, it will take care of us. It is the most precious substance known to all living creatures; therefore, we must cherish it and protect it."

Elias scratched his head and cleared his throat. "So you...and all these beings I have met during my travels...and even Zoltan have already lived longer than any known human. I don't get it."

"Fear and evil have been around since man first walked this planet—so has love. For reasons unknown to us, all those you have named are the embodiment of what makes humans human. But oddly, we may not be humans. We, too, have a burden to carry, and I can only pity Ordak and others who have donned the embodiment of the negative power of humans—but it is not always our own choice."

"Boy, this is heavy stuff," Kelsa said as they both gave a forced smile, and Cimbora barked.

"We cannot choose where or when we will be born, who our parents are, what color our skin is, whether we're a lion, a mouse or an ant—and so on."

"Or a Minotaur or Troll, for that matter," said Elias.

"Some of us are the personification of love—Zoltan and some of us are spirits of a different realm that try to keep humans balanced. Then others are like Ordak—a boil on the goodness of humans," Ambrosia said as she looked out to the crashing waves below.

22
Ordak Arrives

Startled by a ruckus they heard in the distance, Elias and the others heard someone in the courtyard, and by the sound of it, it seemed like they were entering the Temple. Bracing themselves, they heard someone running up the long flight of stairs as the pounding of each footstep slammed hard on each marble step. Suspecting Ordak, Cimbora ran to the stairs, and looking down, he growled as the sounds got louder as the intruder approached the top floor of the Temple.

"Cimbora, c'mon boy, get back here. It might be Ordak." Elias said. Cimbora backed off but not without a few more commanding barks at the unknown disturbance.

Within a moment, Blugwan, who was beaten badly, appeared on the top step and then collapsed. Dripping in his own blood, he was in pain. "I tried Elias, but I couldn't stop him. Forgive me. He is on his way. Luckily, he did not see me escape. He's still a good way away. His power still seems weak, but he is getting stronger, as you can tell by looking at me."

Both Kelsa and Elias ran to him and tried to comfort him.

"Hey, no worries, Blugwan. You are a good friend, and you are safe now," Elias said.

They helped him to the other side of the room, where Kelsa stayed with him and tried the best she could to ease his suffering with bandages that Ambrosia supplied. Kelsa remembered a spell of sorts that the Seraphs would administer to their wounded. She had spent time with the Seraphs and learned much about their culture and customs. They were the only peaceful and thriving community in the Under World. Her attention and care reduced Blugwan's pain and swelling.

Elias stood front and center with his eyes fixed on the stairway. He pulled his dagger from his boot. He felt his body stiffen, and pricks of sweat beads formed on his head. "I know this feeling all too well. But I'm ready."

Like a miniature cyclone, they heard a hollow, windy sound, and it filled the staircase leading up to the chamber room where they guarded the Elixir. "*That* must be Ordak," Elias shouted over the noise.

The whirlwind filled the room, and no more than a few seconds later, Ordak emerged from the dust and debris he had brought with him. A tall, crooked figure dressed only in dark reddish brown filled the opening. His large head was covered by a web of blue and brown veins. He had jagged protrusions starting at the base of his head and cascading down his spine, and his eyes were red and gray slits. Like a lizard, his fingers were webbed all except his index finger, where he wore the large ring of evil.

His eyes reflected his fear of good. With a stone-hard glare, he stood hissing and surveying the area, and when he was done, he turned and locked his glare onto Elias. From behind his long cape came the diminutive Pewton.

"What? I can't believe it. I heard that you had *changed*," Elias said.

With his fingers in his mouth and his shoulders hunched over, Pewton looked to Blugwan and saw that he was semi-conscious but shouted anyway. "Blugwan, tell Elias about Pewton. Please tell. I *have* changed."

"Shut up, you worthless Troll," said Ordak. "If you had changed, you've changed back. You're with me now."

Blugwan woke when he heard the Troll's voice, and with a weak but audible voice, he said, "Elias, Ordak has captured Pewton. It's not what you think."

At that moment, Ordak sent a stream of dark, powerful beams from his fingertip that lifted Blugwan into the air and dropped him on the cold marble floor, rendering him unconscious. Pewton hid his face in his hands and cried.

"Never mind them, Elias. This is about me—and you," Ordak said.

"It's never been about us, Ordak. It has only been about *you* and your slimy, sick ways. Your evil and dark powers all but destroyed you in the past. Haven't you learned?"

"Tsk, tsk, Elias. I just arrived, and you are already jabbing me with petty insults...and yes, I have *learned*, little Elias. I have learned that evil doesn't die; it just changes."

"You are nothing but a petty insult as you lead through fear...by evil ways to get what you want, but you are just a moment too late to steal the Elixir as it is mine to protect. *MINE*."

"A moment too late? Steal? ...and *YOURS*. Really?"

"Look." Ambrosia pointed to the horizon. There was a blue, glowing shadow of a man streaming toward them on nothing but a cloud. Cimbora ran to the balcony and barked.

"Zoltan. Yep, that's him. I can tell. I knew he wouldn't be far away," said Elias.

"He's always medleying where he doesn't belong, that pesky *do-gooder*. He's always been one for a dramatic entrance." Ordak said.

Zoltan's bright blue image softly lofted into the open space, and as he did, his appearance immediately became clear. He stood to the right of Elias and near the balcony. "So Ordak, I'm now a 'pesky do-gooder'? You would make me laugh; however, your ways are tired as you claw your way back to what you think is a prize—to be the Conveyor of All Evil, *really now?* To be *you* must be sad and lonely as you are always looking over your shoulder, and you never know who or what will knock you from your crumbling pedestal."

"You know nothing. Your ways do not work—never have. You are a shriveled-up has-been."

"Oh really, Ordak. Join what is good," said Zoltan, "and you will enjoy the riches that come with it as good does not try to overcome good; rather, good grows even larger and welcomes more good." Zoltan looked over to Elias and Kelsa and said, "I just don't understand why he and all the other fearful, evil beings don't get it." Zoltan grinned and turned to Ordak. "As I have been showing you for eons, it is never too late to become part of the bright light of good. To love. To feel love. Ordak—to love. Why do you resist it?"

Impatient, Ordak looked everywhere but at Zoltan as he spoke. "Are you quite done? My, my, my, how you always drone on and on, weak brother. Why are you here anyway? To protect the weak boy." Ordak burst into a shrieking laughter.

Elias tensed up, and he tightened his lips, keeping back his words. He looked at Zoltan. Zoltan gently lifted his hand to remind Elias that this was not the time to react.

"Elias is, as you are very aware, Ordak, more than capable of taking care of himself. Shall I remind you of what happened not so long ago? In *your* kingdom nonetheless." said Zoltan.

Ordak scowled and hissed.

"When I heard it was you and not Hibush, I told myself I should show up to wish you a proper goodbye, my old haggard friend, that is, if you do not want to join what is good."

"Oh, you must have it all wrong, my dear feeble Zoltan," Ordak said.

"Oh, do I? You should not be here, but somehow, you managed with your last ounce of evil powers to give it one more misguided chance. I give you an 'A+' for 'effort,' but your powers are yesterday's news. The Elixir should never come close to your lips—EVER!" Zoltan's words ended in a crescendo and echoed throughout the room like a boom of a thousand drums.

"Impressive," Ordak mocked Zoltan, and he continued, "I don't know what you are talking about. You do not make the rules for who may partake in the Elixir of Life. The Priestess and her little so-called guardians have been a mere roadblock over the years for so many like me, as you have as well, but now I'm here, and that will all change. Elias is now the only obstacle in my way," Ordak said as he turned and looked at Elias as if he were peering straight through him. "I don't count you as an obstacle, Elias. I view you as a mere gasp of unwanted air."

Ambrosia raised her chin and folded her arms. With an abrupt nod, she brought Ordak to his knees. Quite unexpected, Ordak had rarely been controlled in this manner as his face trembled and arms flaccidly lay to his sides.

"Ambrosia," Elias said, "don't waste your energy as his battle is with me."

Ambrosia walked up to Ordak and looked down at him. "Over the millennia, it has been *his* influence that has created the greedy and power-hungry scavengers who test me and the powers of this Temple. No one has the authority to turn life into a weapon. You disgust me."

She turned and walked away, and when she was about ten feet away, she raised her hand and released her hold on Ordak. He fell to the floor, but he quickly rose and pointed his disgusting gnarly hand toward Ambrosia. However, at that moment, a monstrous rumbling began and shook the Temple. Everyone was thrown off balance, and the vibration was so strong that parts of the walls cracked as the sound was deafening.

Ambrosia spoke up. "I'm afraid, Ordak, that the eighth day is nearing. Unless you have an amazing game plan, you will be going under. And you may not know what happens to those who cannot escape at the last moment of the last day. You may turn into no more than a slug under a rock, but you shall, indeed, live forever—on Eahta."

Rethinking his approach as he knew he was outnumbered, Ordak walked over to the opposite end of the balcony where Zoltan stood, and with his back to all, he spoke so they would hear him. "Never fear Ambrosia. I have all my powers. Your little spell was impressive, but nothing that I can't handle. The Isle of Eahta has been wonderful for my recovery. This place is all about *life* and has done so much for me. All I needed was a few days of the enriching powers of Eahta and, of course, a helping hand from my dear friend. Wouldn't you say, Pewton?"

Standing across the room from Ordak, Pewton grimaced, and at that moment, he let out a cry. "Monster—Ordak, you're a monster!" As fast as he could, he ran toward Ordak with his arms extended, intending to push him off the balcony. Knowing he was in danger, Elias shouted for him to stop, but the Troll continued at full speed, and at the last moment, Ordak stepped aside and tripped Pewton. He careened over the railing to his apparent demise. Kelsa screamed, and Elias rushed toward him. It had been too sudden even for Zoltan to attempt a spell to save the Troll. There was such little time for anyone to react.

Cimbora growled, showing his teeth, and lunged at Ordak. His jaw clamped down with might on his leg, but Ordak waved his bony hand, and Cimbora became tranquil and fell to the floor. Ordak then levitated Cimbora and laughed with demonic delight as he played with him high in the air like a marionette.

Zoltan raised his hand and waved it three times, and Cimbora landed gently on the floor and ran to Elias' side.

"Zoltan to the rescue. You are boring and old, my wonderful but decrepit friend. Don't you have any other tricks up your sleeve? I've seen all of these."

"Enough! Enough, I said," Elias stood between the two old nemeses with his arms extended like a referee in a boxing match.

"Elias, I know the Elixir of Life is around the other side of that curved wall and behind a secret door of some sort. I also know that you have the code to open the door. Let's stop dancing around and tell me what that code would be.

"What? You need a code, Ordak? You are so powerful, but you need this 'little weak' boy's code?" Zoltan said.

"I thought I would try to do this in a civilized fashion, Zoltan. As such, I will gladly share the Elixir with you and all the others here. We shall drink our fill and put our differences to the side. Perhaps I would enjoy the world of—*love*—as I am open to trying something different. Yes, Zoltan, perhaps it is time for me to come to the sweetness and brightness of good."

"Well, if that's the case, Ordak, Elias, give him the code, "said Zoltan.

"What?" Elias raised his hands in awe. Turning to Ordak, he said, "Do you think I'm some kind of idiot?" Just like that? After what you have just done and what you have done over the centuries, you think I'm going to believe that you are ready to find love in your heart? *Now?* You do not even try to be convincing as you mock us. I know what honesty looks like, and it's not your sad face."

"Just what I was hoping you'd say," said Zoltan, nodding as he sat on a stone bench far from Ordak. Elias began to laugh as the others joined in, only making Ordak angrier.

"Elias, time is running out for you, Kelsa, your mangy dog, and the Minotaur slumping over there. I would suggest you cooperate with me before the Isle of Eahta is swallowed up, taking you and the others as it plunges deep into the sea—that is, unless you have an escape hatch of some kind, you do not have *any* bargaining power," Ordak boomed.

Lightning bolts began to fill the sky, and one rumble after another made it hard to hear. More cracks in the wall formed, and dust and debris poured down as parts of the wall crashed around them.

Zoltan stepped up. "Your quarrel is not with the boy."

"No, Zoltan," Elias said, and Zoltan quickly turned his head to where only Elias could see his face. Zoltan winked. Cimbora ran up to Zoltan, and the great sorcerer bent down and rubbed his ears. He whispered to Cimbora. "The Turul is on her way and will bring Elias what he needs."

"Zoltan, you have always been far too good, and it is a wonder you have made it this long," said Ordak.

"Why, thank you—I guess."

"It matters not who succumbs to me; it matters only that I am victorious and leave with the Elixir of Life. But if you insist, you—Zoltan, you and I will duel. The winner gets the Elixir of Life—that means, as only Elias can do, he must open the chamber and watch me drink."

"I was hoping you'd say that. I'll choose the weapons. Swords to the end, and when I say to the end, I mean to the end."

"NO! Zoltan!" Elias said.

"Do not fear Elias. This is the only way. The longer we wait, we will all be doomed."

Within seconds, using a spell, Ordak fashioned a sword from the knotted-up rope that was tied around his waist. Double-sided, the thick dark steel was ornately decorated with dragon wings, and its hilt was barbed with spikes.

"Ow. Why did you do that?" Elias said, rubbing his head after Zoltan plucked a strand of

hair from Elias' crown.

"What else should I have done? I had to think fast—I must forge a new sword."

With a blink of an eye, a sword appeared in Zoltan's hand. The long steel of Zoltan's new sword glimmered a bluish silver and emanated from a simple cross guard to protect his hand.

Clang! Clang! Clang! With metal striking metal, the two began at once as the others looked on. Cimbora dug his nose into Elias' leg and barked. Elias was feeling tense and was keeping his sights on Zoltan and Ordak; he gently pushed his snout away and said, "C'mon, Cimbora, this is life or death. I can't play now."

Cimbora kept barking, and Kelsa said, "Hey Elias, he's trying to tell you something."

Cimbora barked, and Elias realized what he was saying. "Huh? Oh sorry. Okay, the Turul will bring me what I need? I wonder what it is. Hmmm, let's keep a lookout. Thanks, buddy."

Clang! Clang! Clang! Zoltan pirouetted, surprising Ordak as Zoltan landed a stinging blow to Ordak's hilt, making him drop his sword. Not having enough time for a jag, Ordak scooped up his sword, and with freakish rage, he began swinging the blade in a fevered way. *Clang! Clang! Clang!*

Quietly and going undetected, Kelsa and Ambrosia helped Blugwan around to the Chamber door. "This is out of sight to Ordak, and you will both be hidden."

Out of Zoltan and Ordak's view, Elias spoke to Kelsa. "I'm going to open the door, and you, Blugwan, and Cimbora go into the chamber— where the portal is. It will only allow for three of us to go through unless the four of us go fast and before it fades. I plan to go fast! Don't worry about that."

"What? Elias, this is too risky. Let's do it now. We've got to go now! Zoltan will keep Ordak away from the Elixir; I just know it. We've got to get out of here now."

"No Kelsa. I'm the one who has to ensure the safety of the Elixir. It's got to be me. I can't go anywhere."

Ambrosia spoke, "Elias is our only hope. I know what the Turul is bringing you. It is the Sword of Light. The Turul has always been its guardian. The Turul renders it only in extreme cases. It has been wielded by many but by only those who are known to be just and good. By doing so, they have *always* vanquished their evil aggressors."

"Wow. I know Zoltan has a plan. I'm sorry, Kelsa, but I am here to protect the Elixir, and until I know it is in good hands, I can't leave. That's why I came here in the first place. I can't just leave now. Don't worry; we'll make sure everything goes as planned." Elias said.

"I just wish there was another way, Elias."

"Me too, but this is going to work. So I want you all there and ready. I'll close the door so Ordak can't get in, and when it is time, I'll open it and join all of you when the time is right. I will close the door behind me, keeping Ordak away from the Elixir. We'll be on our way home as he sinks with the Isle of Eahta. Zoltan will be able to leave the way he came. It's going to work."

"This must be accomplished by the time you hear the chime of the seventh gong—before it hits eight. This will give you the time you need if you move fast. If not, the portal vanishes, and no one may leave through it," Ambrosia said.

"Okay, so even if I'm not in the chamber, you must go through the portal without me. Promise me."

"Oh Elias, I don't know," said Kelsa.

"Promise me! You must—I will find another way as I have always before. I was told that even with a speck of light, you can find the way. I am not alone, nor have I ever been during my journey. I will find a way."

23
No Regrets

Clang! Clang! Clang! Ordak locked his sword with Zoltan's, their trembling hands only inches apart. They were nose to nose. Sweat streamed from the tops of their heads. Over Ordak's shoulder, Zoltan caught a glimpse of the crimson sky and saw Turul with the Sword of Light in her strong claws. Out of Ordak's sight, the Turul stealthily landed next to Elias, and he took the sword and nodded to the great bird. With a newfound surge of energy, Zoltan disengaged their clenched lock of the swords, and as he did, he faltered backward. Ordak revved back and swung his sword with all his might, striking Zoltan's sword out of his sweaty hands. He stood only an arm's length away from Ordak. Vulnerable, Zoltan had no time to react. Elias, panic-stricken, cried out and ran to him. He was too late, and the evil lord of all darkness, Ordak, jabbed his sword into Zoltan's side. Stunned, he held his bloody side and solemnly crumpled to the marble floor. Ordak hovered tall as a crooked smile filled his face, followed by a creepy, hissing laugh.

"It's over, Zoltan, and being one of high integrity and goodness, you certainly will honor your commitment to me. You, too, Elias," he smirked. "And I expect you to honor me as a new day is upon us." Pointing his sword to the center of the room, he said, "It is time for you to open the chamber."

"Shut up, Ordak!" Elias kneeled by Zoltan, cradling his head.

Ordak backed away, knowing that Elias had the code and he didn't. With time running short, Ordak knew Elias was the only way to get his hands on the Elixir. "You've got a minute to say your goodbyes."

"C'mon Zoltan, get up. We've got work to do. We're not finished here. We're going home soon. You've got lots more to show me."

"Elias, only because of you do I know that my long life is now complete. My work has been for good, for love. I now pass that along to you. My time has come. Your time is now," he said with a warm glow in his eyes.

"No, I don't want *my time*, Zoltan."

"Take your new power on all your journeys and never forget it."

"My new power?"

"Why yes. Light, by boy, light. It solves all that ails our frail humanity. Think about it—the light has been your companion; it has opened your eyes, it has kept you warm, and it has helped you in all the darkness you have seen. Light is love."

"You can't go, Zoltan."

"I will travel to be with Tas to the Land That Doesn't Exist and to be among the Dancing Souls. I will forever be part of the light—your light. What a marvelous thought, don't you agree?"

Elias, tight-lipped, reluctantly nodded. His eyes welled up.

"So, you see, I will never be too far from you, my dear boy. You are ready—you make me so happy."

"Don't go, Zoltan...don't go."

Zoltan reached up and put his trembling palm on his cheek. Tears filled their eyes. "Like the little water bug, you have climbed the stem. My boy, you have climbed the stem. Oh yes, rest for a moment, but then stretch your wings and fly Elias, fly and don't look back. You will grow, and your flight will open you to all in the cosmos."

"I don't want the cosmos, Zoltan, I want you."

"It is time. You have been chosen."

"Chosen? I don't want to be chosen."

"You, my boy, deserve so much, but ordinary as they are, my words, deeds, and love are my gift to you—a gift any grandfather would be honored to give their grandson." He smiled.

"Grandson? You're my..."

"Yes. I love you so."

"I love you, Zoltan—I mean Grand Dad." But why me? Why was I chosen?"

"Why not you? It's part of who you are—always." Zoltan closed his eyes.

Elias gently brushed Zoltan's long white hair from his cheek. His muscles drooped, and his head bent as he closed his eyes. His face was awash with tears. Then, like the screech of a thousand bats, he heard the sick laughter of Ordak.

"So you had your touching moment. Now get up and open the chamber," he roared.

It was then that several rumbles came from different directions and grew in intensity. The Temple shook as Ordak lost his balance. Feeling his adrenaline flow, Elias exploded from where he was and raced to grab the Sword of Light that was hidden from Ordak. A moment later, after the dust and debris ceased its torrent from every side, Elias looked back to Zoltan, but he was replaced with a single ray of pure white light. Confused but abruptly thrown into the danger he now faced, he had to refocus on stopping Ordak and stood ready to battle.

"Ha! You are going against your word, Elias. You are nothing but a low life."

"No, I never promised you anything, Ordak. And neither did my grandfather. You said it—this is a new day, and you are on the dark side of it." With that, Elias plunged toward Ordak with the long tip of the sword. "You are right, Ordak; this *is* about you and me, as you have just made it so."

Retreating, Ordak raised his sword. "You are such a weak boy. Zoltan is gone, and you want to avenge his honor. How dear."

"You are such an evil, fear-mongering coward, and you stand for nothing other than yourself. You will put life in the balance to gain all the power you want."

Clang! Clang! Clang!

"Balance? Life doesn't work that way. It's about accumulating, so if the scale is tipped in my favor, so be it."

"What! You think you know everything, Ordak, but you know nothing."

Clang! Clang! Clang!

"And you, all of sixteen, know so very much, do you?" He twirled and raised his sword.

"It's not that I know so much; it's what I *do* know, I know." *Clang! Clang!*

"Sounds like your grandfather."

Clang! Clang! Clang!

"Compliments will get you nowhere."

"Enough!" Ordak swung with a ferocious blow, striking Elias' sword—the Sword of Light, but it did not flinch, and Elias stood his ground, unaffected by the impact. His stern face flashed a quick smile, and Elias then swung the blade with swift speed and force. As he did, a blinding glow surrounded the blade. Unbalanced, Ordak fumbled backward, and like he was holding an iron-clad anchor, his arm dropped.

The first gong was struck, and the echo took a dozen seconds to fade away.

SHA-BOOONG

Elias looked back at Ambrosia, and she nodded to him, signaling that the three were safe. He knew he had to hurry if he was going to join them in time.

Ordak lurched closer to Elias. Elias raised his sword and took a forceful swing at Ordak. *Clang! Clang! Clang!* Elias and Ordak fought, striking blow after blow. Elias felt nothing as Ordak was showing more and more fatigue.

SHA-BOOONG

Like the weight of all those who wielded the Sword of Light, Ordak felt a force he was unequipped to control. *Clang!*

SHA-BOOONG

Spinning Ordak in circles, Elias landed a blow on Ordak's sword, snapping it in two. The force sent him collapsing to the marble floor. He lost what was left of his weapon as it slid away upon impact and landed across the room. Seeing fear for the first time on his face, Elias stood over Ordak with the point of the blade over his heart. As if all stood still, he counted the remaining bangs of the gong, leaving the Conveyor of All Evil pinned down without any possibilities.

SHA-BOOONG

Elias peered down at his adversary and firmly held the sword, barely resting it on Ordak's chest. For Ordak, each second seemed like an hour.

SHA-BOOONG

Knowing three more gongs were coming, he lifted the sword over his head, and with all his strength, he lunged it toward Ordak and stabbed the fiery point just inches to the side of his head, cutting deep and cracking the marble floor. Ordak's eyes pinched closed. Stupefied, he opened them.

SHA-BOOONG

"I'm not going to end your crummy existence. I want you to get what you want—what

you came for—to live forever. To live as the lowliest creature under a rock here on the Isle of Eahta. Isn't that what you wanted—to live forever?

"You are just a coward, Elias. You have me, but you can't bring yourself to finish me off.

You're too good and don't have what it takes to make it in a dark and cold world."

Still standing over Ordak, Elias said, "Coward? Too good, huh? I'll take that any day, especially today. Remember, I'm an artist. Call it poetic justice, but leaving you to live out your life seems more fitting for you. I'm headed home.

SHA-BOOONG

"Gotta run Ordak. Enjoy your stay." Elias ran to the chamber door where Ambrosia was standing. The floor quaked as Ordak leaped to his feet and began running to the chamber, but Eahta roared like a lion as the Temple walls fell inward. Enormous marble blocks smashed at Ordak's feet and exploded on impact. A gigantic piece of the wall crashed all around him, blocking him from getting any closer to the chamber door. Shrieking, he found himself imprisoned and could not escape the mounds that circled him.

SHA-BOOONG.

The eighth gong sounded, and Elias placed the tip of his index finger on the exact point. "SEVENTY-TWO," he shouted.

The chamber door opened, but he was a moment too late. He watched the colors of the portal fade away before he could act. He felt a rock in the pit of his stomach, and he turned to Ambrosia. "Ambrosia, I have done what I have come here to do. The Elixir of Life has been protected from evil. As you told me when I met you, I could turn around and leave then, but I didn't, as I had come to fulfill a charge that only I could accomplish. I don't have any regrets."

Ambrosia forced a smile. The walls continued to collapse around them.

"I will never leave the Isle of Eahta as you warned." A thunderous rumble vibrated the Temple.

"This time, Elias, you are wrong," Ambrosia approached Elias, and she placed her soft, warm palm on his cheek.

"What do you mean?"

"I will take you to your boat and the portal that led you here. We've got to act *now*."

"What? How?"

"You will see. In just a moment, you will know what you need to do." Just then, Ambrosia transfigured and became the sea serpent he met earlier. Elias jumped on her back and wrapped his arms around her neck as she glided to the balcony. She dove over as the Temple was imploding. They landed in the sea and swam away.

24
Epilogue

As she did most days, Nattymama tended to her garden that surrounded her bungalow and walked to her spot to rest. She sat on a stone bench near the stream. This was her favorite place to reflect on the matters that meant a great deal to her. All was quiet except for the sound of the bubbling and gushing sounds of the water over the flat stones that did little to impede its flow. Like all that surrounded her, pure in essence, she inhaled all that nature had to share. The day was over, and the sun was just beginning to dip over the mountains. Ribbons of color filled the sky, and the sight and scents filled her with joy.

"Nattymama! Nattymama, where are you?"

She remained silent, but the corners of her mouth began to curl up. Out of breath, Elias bounded from her back door, through her herb garden, and down the grassy hill. He came from behind, leaned over, and gently placed his arms around her, hugging her. She raised her thin and arthritic hand, placed it on his, and turned to see his face. "You are back, Elias, you are back! Come. Come sit next to me. Sit next to your Nattymama."

Elias sat next to her, and Nattymama, again, reached out to hold his hand and patted it with her other. Tears welled up in Elias' eyes, and he looked away to the stream.

"What is it? You've had a long journey. You can tell your Nattymama."

"First, is Kelsa and Cimbora—and Blugwan okay?"

"Oh, they are fine. They should be here soon from their hike into the village. And you should see *that* Blugwan—what a looker."

"Blugwan? What?" Elias was stunned by her description.

"Why yes, Minotaurs are not Minotaurs in this realm."

"Oh, that's good to know." Feeling a sense of relief, Elias suddenly became sullen. Trembling, he looked at Nattymama. "Zoltan...Zoltan is..."

"I know, my precious Elias, I know. It was his time."

"Is it true? I mean, is he really my grandfather?"

"Oh yes, he is, and I might add that he is very proud of you. You know you are the spitting image of him when he was all of sixteen—but you're a tad more handsome." Nattymama said with a bit of a giggle.

"Oh, Nattymama." Elias turned red and looked to the horizon. The moment stood still as they both gazed off into the distance.

"You know Elias, his light will always be with us. When we look at the night sky, we will see him in the stars and the moon. We will see him in our dreams. In the sunbeams, we will feel his warmth and see with clarity. Even in the flickering candlelight, the roaring fire, or the teeniest, tiniest speck of light, he is with us. Most of all, Elias, he is in our hearts."

Elias took the heel of his hand and wiped his eyes, and Nattymama pulled him closer.

"He said he was going to be with Tas in the Land that Doesn't Exist. I don't really understand, Nattymama—I was there. Why is it called that?"

"Yes, I know you were there. Think back to when you were preparing to go on your first journey. I said the world is divided into thirds: the Upper World, Middle World, and Under World. You have seen all three. Rarely do we get that very special opportunity to see the Upper World, but you did. You saw what the world could be, but humans—ahhh, they get in the way. Ha! That is why it is called The Land that Doesn't Exist."

"And the Dancing Souls are the light that is in all of us?"

"Indeed. The light in our hearts never dims. Never. The amulet you wear around your neck reminds you of that unique light that is all yours, and that light glows brightest when we are our true selves."

"Thanks, Nattymama." Elias gave her a tight lip smile. "Oh, before I forget, I have something for you."

"You do—I love surprises."

"It's nothing big, but here's something I've never seen before." Elias reached into his pocket and pulled out the beautiful shell he found on the silky-white beach.

"Oh Elias, how beautiful. It is a work of art—much like your wonderful paintings....and much like you."

"You're just saying that."

"You know Nattymama. I don't ever *just* say anything."

Elias nodded and thumped the heel of his hand on this forehead, and they chuckled. "I'd never been to a place like that before. It seemed beautiful and peaceful, but so much was stirring under its surface. So much power and forces that should be left alone."

"Yes, Elias. You described the Isle of Eahta to a tee, but what you described is in each of us as well. Under our beautiful exterior, which we all have, we are a mystery. We must know how to express our own powers to the world—but such force should always be for good."

"You know Nattymama, I just wanted to get home. I belong here. I missed time in the hills with my paints and the beauty I saw... and wanted to see."

"You must get back to it. But Elias, let me tell you a secret."

Elias perked up. "I love your secrets, Nattymama."

"This is important...wherever you are, that's where you belong. The demands of life never stop, and we are called to do many things at different times of life. But when we hear the call and do not answer, we will live a life of regret."

Elias nodded and smiled.

"Elias, there's no telling what your next journey might be, but what I do know is that you will have another call to adventure and another... and another."

"I was afraid you were going to say that."

"Yes, we all aim and hope for a clear path to travel down our whole life, but there is one thing I do know: those paths are made only for fools. That is not for me or you. There is always a bump, a fork or a detour, a cave to explore, and the cool water of a sea we didn't even know existed. If we are true to ourselves, respect where we've been, but keep moving forward, we will feel a sense of gratitude—of joy. That's what *it* is all about.

What do you mean, *it*?

"Life."

They looked, again, to the peaks of the mountain range as the many colorful fingers of the setting sun flickered. With a half-smile but with dry eyes, he turned and looked at Nattymama. She turned to him, and their eyes met. "I will still miss him."

"As you should, my boy...and I will too, Elias, I will too. One day, our lights will join his, and we will all shine brighter, but until then, stay humble and compassionate. Above all, be true to yourself. You're a dragonfly, Elias, so fly. Let your actions be your light."

AUTHOR'S NOTE

There is no statue in this world to honor Elias, as it should be. As it is with Elias, one day, we all become just an idea, a thought, a feeling. Our presence, for good or bad, is, however, imprinted in the cosmos, like it or not. I call this imprint a vibration, as every molecule has an energy and one that is never destroyed. Like a star's light, we see the vibration of its glow billions of years after its light in the physical world has all but been extinguished. The light brings joy.

Oh, he's still around...oh yes. Think of it this way—people come in and out of our lives and serve a purpose. Sometimes, we pay attention, and other times, we may not. It's best to pay attention and to live in that moment as others give us gifts, but we must be ready to accept the gift. Those gifts are rarely wrapped in paper with a bow, but these gifts are remembered and live in our hearts. As Elias learned, it is best to follow your heart, as those who merely follow a dream may be led down a path and get lost, but when you follow your heart—and are true to yourself—your dream is sure to follow.

ABOUT THE AUTHOR

E.G. Kardos, is a literary and fantasy fiction writer, and is the author of five books.

Spirituality, friendship, love, and our connection to the beauty of the universe inspire his writing.

He grew up loving fantasy and couldn't get enough of it whether that be in books, movies, or in play. Art in all forms continues to be important to his creative spirit.

An avid "student" of Joseph Campbell, he is fascinated by the hero's journey as this type of storytelling is embedded in all cultures over thousands of years. THE ELIAS CHRONICLES are true to form as he explores what's most important in our lives today with the mythology and magic that are the fabric of who we are as a people.